The Director

ALEXANDER AHNDORIL is one of Sweden's most celebrated, dynamic and original younger writers, the author of eight novels and ten plays, as well as short stories, essays and screenplays. This is his English debut.

SARAH DEATH has translated works by many Swedish writers including Kerstin Ekman, Sven Lindqvist, and Ellen Mattson. She was awarded the Swedish Academy's 2008 Translation Prize, and has twice won the George Bernard Shaw Prize for translation from Swedish.

From the international reviews of *The Director*:

'A Scandinavian version of Fellini's 'Eight and a Half', the novel melts the imagined and remembered. It also catches the physical atmosphere of Sweden, both warming and chill – like Bergman's relationships.'
Financial Times

'Lovely, poetic prose.' *Metro*

'The language is precise, every word carefully weighed. Seventeen years in the honing, the novel created a furore on publication in Sweden, where Bergman vented his displeasure on national television... It is a sometimes comic, sometimes tragic, always surprising novel that constantly blurs the lines between reality and fantasy.' *Swedish Book Review*

'Ahndoril has produced a novel that is austere and insightful, much like its subject's great works of art.' *The List*

'Is *The Director* a satire or an homage, a parricide in the name of art or a love letter? It is, of course, both. And that is what makes it so rich.' *Svenska Dagbladet*

'*The Director* is a seriously entertaining page-turner about a father and a son, about dream and reality, art and everyday life. It is not only the scandalous novel of this season, but also one of the most outstanding.' *City*

The Director

Alexander Ahndoril
Translated from the Swedish by Sarah Death

First published by Portobello Books Ltd 2007
This paperback edition published 2008

Portobello Books Ltd
Twelve Addison Avenue
Holland Park
London WII 4QR, UK

First published in the original Swedish by Albert Bonniers Förlag as
Regissören in 2006.

The publication of this book was generously supported by the Anglo-Swedish
Literary Foundation

A CIP catalogue record is available from the British Library

9 8 7 6 5 4 3 2 1

ISBN 978 1 84627 048 2

www.portobellobooks.com

Designed by Nicky Barneby

Typeset in Imprint MT by Avon DataSet Ltd, Bidford on Avon, Warwickshire

Printed in Great Britain by CPI Bookmarque, Croydon, CR0 4TD

For Saga, Julia and Nora

1

So now, even the melancholy light of a night in high summer is captured in a glass jar, thinks Ingmar.

And sees a white road flowing like water past shadow-soft houses.

A man of his own age walks towards him, quivers and all at once is twenty paces closer.

He seems to be dressed as a priest.

Light spills out, sucks back and disappears through a window that has swung open.

A woman with goose-pimpled arms fastens the catch. She goes back across the room, passing the shade of the standard lamp, and sits down on the edge of the bed.

Whispers start running through the hot metal of the projector. Or perhaps they have only become audible now Ingmar has turned off the lamp.

He lingers, intending to go out the back way, through the projection room door.

Doesn't want to see anybody.

Can't face explaining that he must finish work on the Stravinsky before he can turn his mind to the new script.

Ingmar emerges into the afternoon darkness, feels the cold in his eyes, around his sweaty neck and deep inside his nose.

Dry snow slips down the tin roof of the Little Studio, twenty metres above, falls past the string of black windows and lands on the outside steps with muffled thuds.

Swinging light from a lantern skitters its way along the brick wall and abruptly illuminates his face: tense forehead, eyebrows, the deep furrow cutting a curved line from the side of his nose, down past the corner of his mouth.

Softly in the wind, fine-grained snow spreads like a scratchy film across the road, round the corner and along the damp-damaged concrete of the office building.

He continues upstream. Feels the icy bite of the air around his ankles and up his trouser legs.

Just as Ingmar passes the downpipe and drain, a window opens.

He turns round.

A naked arm makes a swift movement along the window frame.

And behind the shifting light on the glass there's the glimpse of a face. A woman, her mouth open. She must have called out to him.

A brief exchange of words with a technician in the corridor. About the company's huge screening room, the cinema known as the Opera House. The new loud-speaker system is still crackling, Ingmar says.

The secretary's cigarette smoke lingers in the darkness of the boss's office; a pale drift across Dymling's chair and the ivory-coloured, enamelled desk lamp, the folders and filing cabinets.

There's virtual silence. The walls are creaking slightly. Someone is moving in the corridor by the duplicating room.

He picks up the pale grey telephone receiver.

'Bergman.'

Dymling clears his throat and mutters that the secretary thought he'd gone home at three.

'I sneaked off to the Opera House,' answers Ingmar.

The boss tries to hide his irritation as he says you can't waste all your time on opera when there's a film to be made. Ingmar doesn't correct the misunder-standing, since Dymling is in fact right that it's the opera production which is holding up the promised script.

He looks at the little splashes of colour on the window pane, the cracked frame and white plastic sill.

The oar stroke drags up a sleepy movement in the yellow water, a trailing thread. And out of the darkness black leaves come rising, tumbling around like faces in the light.

Strangers and friends.

His little sister Nitti opening her mouth as wide as she can.

He and his father rotate softly, are sucked down and into the shadow under the rowing boat. While a doctor with thin eyebrows rises slowly. Followed by Dymling, who smiles as he says he hopes for one last summer after all.

The doctor has no time to answer before the oar blade cuts the water and the leaves are dragged down into a powerful eddy.

Ingmar perches on the edge of his desk and follows their stately twirling with his gaze.

Wet footprints on the fitted carpet lead right up to him.

Dymling holds the receiver away from his mouth while he coughs.

Ingmar unfastens his lined overcoat, sniffs to stop his nose running. A vein extends from the bridge of his nose and divides like a forking road in the centre of his forehead.

The telephone rings behind Ingmar's back as he walks down the corridor. His hand gropes for support on the dusty ledge above the panelling.

The icy wind disarranges his combed hair; black strands are blown over his eyes.

A grey car turns squeakily out of the tall gates and disappears.

Ingmar holds his coat closed with his hands in the pockets and walks as fast as he can without letting in too much cold air.

A plastic bag filled with air scuds across the road.

Ingmar screws up his eyes and moves slowly on.

Something big, like a leaden grey sail, towers above the cars in the gloomy car parking place.

He comes to a halt, takes one more step and pushes his fringe out of his eyes.

It's an enormous schoolroom blackboard. Maybe three metres tall, with supporting struts. A wet trail of melted snow is running down one side.

Ingmar goes up to it and takes a piece of chalk from the ledge, draws a childish horse and writes 'Max' above it.

He blows on his hands, then draws a speech bubble coming from the horse's mouth: 'Are we filming this autumn?' it asks.

'Yes,' answers Ingmar, putting the chalk back on the ledge. 'I've almost finished the script.'

He gets into the car, pulls the door shut and drums his fingertips on the steering wheel.

'Well, what the hell,' he whispers.

Behind the big blackboard, beyond the low fence round the car park, stands a real horse. It is silhouetted against the thick tangle of branches. It sidesteps heavily, moving closer to the trees, muscles quivering.

Ingmar thinks of Max, standing in front of the car with his hands clamped under his arms and saying he's been offered the role of Faust in Uppsala in October.

'You'll have to turn it down.'

The horse slips on the frozen slope. Its right gaskin and hock tense to counteract the sudden loss of footing. Against the dark trees the heavy head tosses, the body regains its balance and moves backwards, angular and jerky.

* * *

Wearing the dark grey sweater that's white on the reverse side, Ingmar carries his cup of hot milk from the kitchen to the dining table.

The Hogarth etching on the wall is reflected in the window. It extends far out across the garden and the dark field like a horizontal slide.

Ingmar looks at the earliest notes, when the film was going to be about a priest who shuts himself up in a church and tells God he's going to stay there until He shows himself, no matter how long it takes.

Ingmar knows he'll soon have to get started on the script, but repeats to himself that there's absolutely no hurry.

He's got to keep calm.

Has no choice but to wait for his subject, let it hatch at its own glutinous pace.

*

Not really feeling restless, he wanders from room to room, puts the gramophone record of the *Symphony of Psalms* by the telephone and all of a sudden remembers a pale grey night in the vicarage by the Sophia Hospital.

His mother had come home after her convalescence at Duvnäs and was crying frantically in her room.

Ingmar was lying in bed, unable to sleep.

Distant thuds – like someone chopping wood – carry him with them, further into memory.

His mother called through the door that his father wasn't to come in. His footsteps traipsed back and forth along the passage and his voice grumbled. What is it, Karin? Kai dear, what's the matter?

Followed by the sudden thumps, the screams and threats.

Then once again the footsteps back and forth and his mother's crying, increasingly apathetic.

As softly as knitting stitches unravelling, Ingmar creeps in to see if his little sister has woken up.

She's sitting in bed staring straight ahead, at the tapestry from Dalarna.

Her light-suffused skin and anxious mouth.

He sits down beside her and starts to play with Rosenblom, her doll. A young earl who assumes everyone he meets is a servant. He tries to persuade a crocodile to help him get his trunk across the river.

Nitti laughs into the pillow.

Rosenblom thinks it's just an awkward misunderstanding when the crocodile (instead of taking the trunk) grabs his leg and starts dragging him down the steep riverbank.

Then the floor gives a sudden creak and there are steps approaching. An iron ball rolling in their direction. Ingmar hides behind the linen cupboard; his father strides heavily into the room, sits on the edge of the bed and puts his hands over his ears although there isn't a sound. And without a word, he rests his great head in Nitti's lap.

The ornamental clock gives a dry tick and braces itself, but all that follows is a faint resonance within the closed wooden body.

Ingmar dials number after number, waits for the swift return of the dial, then listens to the long tones.

The receiver is lifted from its cradle and there is silence.

Then his father clears his throat and answers as he always has done.

Presumably he's sitting at his desk, where the framed photographs stand, without undoing his jacket. His father never so much as loosens his narrow tie, even though he is alone in the study.

'I waited until seven,' Ingmar says. 'So you'd have half an hour to rest after your meal.'

'Ah, well, thank you very much,' he laughs, embarrassed.

Ingmar stops biting his thumbnail and asks if his parents are busy: if they have guests, or are watching Hyland's *Warm Welcome*.

'I didn't forget to thank you for the television, did I?' his father asks.

Did he really think I felt he hadn't been grateful enough, writes Ingmar in the margin of the novel, but doesn't end the sentence with a question mark, simply carries on reading about the abrupt silence left by his lack of answer, about the way the turned-down neck of his sweater looked like a clerical collar reflected in the dining room window.

His father clears his throat. He creaks his body against the back of the chair. Announces in a formal voice that Dag rang from Ankara this morning.

'Well, how are things with him?'

'I don't know,' he replies. 'Your big brother seems content to be an embassy secretary and you seem . . .'

'I was really thinking about his leg,' interrupts Ingmar, but immediately regrets it.

'I'll fetch Mother – she was the one who spoke to Dag.'

'There's no need,' Ingmar says quickly. 'What I mean is, it's nice to have a chance to talk to you, Father.'

There are headlights beyond the dark field, filtering unevenly through the avenue of trees.

Ingmar fiddles with the soft corner of the record cover, with a flap of the plastic inner sleeve, and asks his father if they have decided yet whether to spend the summer anywhere in particular.

'Weren't you maybe thinking of renting – what's their name – Sidenwalls' house again?'

'Yes,' says his father, his thoughts elsewhere.

'That suited you quite well, didn't it?'

'Possibly,' he mumbles.

Ingmar, feeling stressed, scratches his scalp.

'I thought it did.'

'If I can't get to the sea and the islands it's all the same to me.'

'Yes, but I've had an offer – you might say – of a summer cottage on Torö Island that you could take.'

'No,' replies his father with a smile in his voice.

'It would be perfect for you both.'

'Thanks, but . . .'

Ingmar can hear his father getting up, stretching the telephone lead and opening the door to the drawing room a little way.

Ingmar bites his thumbnail, looks at it and chews a bit more.

'I suppose it will be time for a new film soon,' says his father in an effort to make conversation as he looks past the pleated fabric screen, along the rows of book spines and over to the double doors.

'Yes, it's opening at the Röda Kvarn cinema in October.'

'That will please your mother.'

'But now I'm writing a completely new film that might interest you, Father – it's going to be about a priest.'

'Not about me, I hope.'

'I haven't got that far.'

'And Mother said something about an opera, too.'

'You'd both be really very welcome to come to the opening night; it would make me very happy,' he says.

'You had better talk to Mother about it.'

'Stravinsky's actually going to . . .'

Ingmar can hear a voice saying something in the background. Father replies that it's Putte and passes the telephone over.

'Has anything happened?' his mother asks.

'Something terrible,' replies Ingmar. 'I asked whether the two of you wanted to come to the opening night of *The Rake's Progress*.'

'At the Opera House?'

'I mean, it's nothing special, but . . . Do you think Father might want to?'

'And what about Mother?'

'But seriously, do you think he's interested?'

'Yes, but you know what he's like,' she says.

'Nobody's forcing him,' Ingmar sighs, getting to his feet. 'I'm not going to waste my time wheedling or . . .'

'Ingmar, Ingmar,' she interrupts calmly. 'I just don't want you to be disappointed.'

'I already am.'

'You mustn't say that.'

'What? What mustn't I say?'

'Don't be . . .'

'You don't damn well need to protect . . .'

'That's enough,' she says sharply. 'I don't want to hear anything about . . .'

'Forget the whole bloody idea, then.' shouts Ingmar, slams down the receiver and wrenches at the lead to pull the plug out of the socket. The telephone falls to the floor with a crash and a feeble ring of its bell. He gives it a kick, but already feels distanced from his anger and leaves the room.

His hand shaking, Ingmar moves the needle over the dark water, the undulating surface, then stands listening to the confined sway of the oboe before the spring wells up.

A skin has formed on the milk in the mug on the dining table. He looks at the yellow notepad, but realizes he can't even make himself sit down. In a mood more of jealousy than annoyance, he returns to the memory of his father's large head in his little sister's lap. He hadn't thought his father capable of such a gesture, seeking affection. He lay there with his eyes closed, talking quite calmly about his time as priest at the Forsberga ironworks.

There's a scratch on the record and the needle jumps back: now it's Rosenblom the doll coming into the room instead, pale-faced. He goes and lies down with his head in Nitti's lap. She thinks he has his eyes shut and is falling asleep; she doesn't realize he's still staring his black stare.

The needle is dislodged from its groove again: Dag pulls one of the doll's arms off and holds up the trembling body to show Nitti.

Ingmar goes over to the gramophone and shifts the needle to the next movement: 'I longed so terribly for a little sister for Dag,' his father says, 'that in the end Mother made a little girl out of fabric and put it on my bed on our wedding anniversary'.

'A doll?'

'Yes, but then she got pregnant as well,' he says, a tired smile spreading across his whole face.

'With me?' asks Nitti without thinking.

Ingmar opens the larder door again and rummages among the packets. The oats fall to the floor with a soft thud, Ingmar takes a step back and wipes the sweat from his top lip. He's baffled, wonders if Käbi was hungry and took the chocolate with her to the airport.

He looks at the grey oats and remembers he

finished off the chocolate himself, at four o'clock in the morning. As he sat there with a splitting headache, listening to Leinsdorf's runny version of *The Rake's Progress*. So now I won't have anything for tonight, he tells himself. When I can't sleep and can't write. When I'm trying to stop myself ringing the hotel in Bremen.

He does up his jacket on the way out to the car, climbs into the cold seat, pulls out the choke, starts the engine and moves off down the drive between green rhododendron bushes. The drive crunches under the tyres. He turns onto the road, changes gear and accelerates cautiously. The beams of the headlights create a corridor between the black gardens.

He drums on the steering wheel, bites his bottom lip and suddenly sees a coin at the end of the tunnel of light.

On a bed of grey sand under knee-deep water.

Or in a misty glass jar.

It gives a faint flicker, just before the image comes up on the stamped surface.

It's a young woman in traditional Thüringian folk costume. She's lying asleep in a meadow while the thundery sky casts its trembling, sickly yellow light on her.

She wakes and sits up.

Oblivious to that person panting like a big dog. The blunt claws clattering over the parquet flooring.

The woman simply gets up, stretches out her arms and swings round. But she suddenly stops short, looks frightened and hurries away from the meadow just as two roe deer stream across the road and vanish again.

Ingmar can feel the racing pulse in his temples as he reduces his speed. The car almost skids on the steep bend. He scratches his head with the stress of it all. Tries to pull himself together by thinking about the new film. Tells himself he's got to get away from the mystifications of the last one; he doesn't want the priest to see his God crawling out of the wallpaper.

I'm tempted by the purity of a chamber play, he thinks, and repeats the words to himself.

The whole plot will be played out in real time: Sunday, the summoning bell, a priest too tired to go on claiming he believes in God.

Starts to realize he never really has.

For him, the service is an unbearable ritual, completely drained of meaning.

Just as it always has been for me.

I want to tell the story of a priest who is only doing his job.

I want to tell the story of myself, he thinks, if I had given in to the expectation that I would become a priest.

The kiosk in the square at Djurholm is shut, its bright green wooden shutters closed and padlocked. Elastic streaks of snow go winding across the empty paving stones. He sits parked at the roadside, keeps the car engine running. Wonders what he's doing. He ought to go back to the house and ring Käbi before it gets too late. Ought to cook some dinner. Ought to sit in his study and write. He taps the steering wheel slowly with his hand, stops after a while, leans back and remembers he's got some chocolate at his work flat.

In the cupboard above the draining board.

There's no pause for deliberation before he sets off to drive to Stockholm.

* * *

Ingmar locks himself in, eases off his shoes and goes into the kitchenette; he opens the cupboard door, sees a packet of dark chocolate coins on the shelf, closes the cupboard and goes to the window.

Blows on his hands.

The snow melts on the window sills here, Ingmar thinks, and looks down into the street. A rusty railing against a concrete wall. Lying in the back of a yellow tipper truck there's a road sign that has been dug up, with a conical concrete base.

He looks towards the crossroads at Karlaplan, sees where the pavement has been taken up. The piles of snow-covered paving stones. The vibrating reflections along the bright yellow ribbon of plastic.

*

His body heavy, he lies down on the bed and thinks he'll take a walk to Gärdet and look at the new Broadcasting Centre tomorrow. They're already transferring staff from Kungsgatan.

He rings the Bremen Hilton.

It isn't far from the concert hall, Die Glocke, Käbi said.

She'll be playing four romantic pieces – Brahms, Chopin, Schubert, Schumann – in the small auditorium in a couple of hours and her voice is strangely calm.

Beside the pale grey telephone on the bedside table stands a white alarm clock. The back with its curved copper rosette lying flat, two ribbed knobs. A water glass with thin rings of limescale where the water has evaporated.

'I think it's you who sounds odd,' says Käbi with sudden weariness. 'Are you at home?'

'Yes,' he answers, to avoid having to explain his car journey.

A rectangle still opens its shadowy window in the faded, medallion-patterned wallpaper where the photograph hung before it was knocked from its frame onto the floor.

'What is it then?' asks Käbi.

'Nothing, well . . . I spoke to Father on the phone, thought I'd invite him to the first night, but . . . I don't know.'

'Did you have an argument?'

'No, it's just . . . I tried to explain the new film to . . .'

'But why do a thing like that?' she interrupts him. 'Really? You know it's ridiculous. He's never liked your films.'

'I don't know anything of the kind,' says Ingmar. 'And I don't give a damn. I hope he hates my films.'

'No you don't.'

'It always comes down to how chronically disapproving of his sons the old man is. And he really is, you know. He just can't fathom why we didn't go into the church. What we do is totally bloody worthless.'

'Yes.'

'I think that's why I've got to make a film about myself as a priest,' Ingmar says. 'To show him what it would look like. How happy everybody would be.'

'But who knows how it would turn out?' she says. 'Maybe I'd be a little vicar's wife.'

'Mmm, except that I killed off the wife last night.'

'While I lay sleeping,' she jokes.

'I decided to have the vicar's wife die a few years earlier. That was what made him lose his faith, or whatever you want to call it.'

'So now there are no women in the film?'

'Oh yes, there's a teacher – she's his lover.'

'Who will you get to . . .'

'I thought . . .'

'Pardon?'

'I thought Ingrid could play her.'

'Isn't she too beautiful for that role?'

Ingmar gently presses his own stomach, the fragile emptiness, the dull response to his touch, the answering spasm.

'You sound a bit tired,' she says. 'Have you had anything to eat?'

'I haven't had time to cook . . .'

But there ought to be some fillet of veal in the fridge – can you go and check?'

'No, I . . .'

'Go on. I'll wait.'

Ingmar puts down the receiver, and stupidly enough goes and looks in the empty refrigerator in the kitchenette, calls out that she was right, comes back and mutters that he's put the oven on.

'But I was just going to say I remembered I'd thrown out what was left.'

'I must have seen something else, then.'

A dog barks, down on the pavement.

'You're not at home, are you?'

'Yes I am.'

Someone runs across the floor in the flat above, slams the door.

Ingmar turns the alarm clock round, sees the finger marks on the glass. Thinks of the pictures his father always kept on his bedside table.

His own mother and Nitti. Never his wife. Never his sons.

*

In the middle of their conversation about the musical atmosphere in *The Rake's Progress* and the chorus of prostitutes in the second scene, after a brief pause, a thoughtful moment, Käbi suddenly says she wants him to tell her as soon as he falls in love with another woman.

'What do you mean?' he asks, trying to sound amused and surprised.

Along the connecting lines of the telephone, the breathless splices, the swell of distance, Ingmar suddenly hears a movement in Käbi's hotel room, like paws across metal, a cautious sprinkling over a wet carpet.

'I just get the feeling something's starting to happen,' she says calmly. 'I notice it in myself when I'm away travelling.'

'What do you notice?'

'Mmm, well . . . when we first met,' she says, 'everything had a romantic shimmer, which was quite erotic – wasn't it? But one has to move on from that feeling . . . and it needn't be a change for the worse, as you often say. Because we've got something now that's much more real. And I agree, but after my trip to Bordeaux I was a bit scared, because I actually think your need for affairs is much greater than mine.'

'What's happened, Käbi?'

'Nothing,' she answers. 'I happened to meet Sviatoslav Richter and realized I was enjoying myself, finding it exciting I mean.'

'Have you jumped into bed with that . . .'

'Stop it,' she said. 'I'd never be unfaithful to you.'

'But if you did, you'd lie about it.'

'We had dinner at this Le Jardin place, blah blah blah.'

'And then? You had dinner. What did you do afterwards?'

2

We had sex after we'd switched off the bedside lights, thinks Ingmar.

As thoroughly blind as if we'd had our eyes closed, we reached out for each other.

In the unstable darkness.

Deep beneath the fading tones of the evening's extravagance: the curved balconies, boxes and rolling floors of the Opera House.

Käbi tried to whisper something about what was already so obvious to both of them, lifting her bottom as she did so.

Ingmar was careful, almost businesslike, as he pushed up her batiste nightdress.

Both suddenly aglow.

And yearningly oppressed by the awareness that a child could be conceived if they went on – they went on, without spoken agreement.

Quietly, tightly entwined.

He can see this through the film of water between two plates of glass, through a misted jam jar, through the great glasshouse at night, a block of ice filled with light.

Across the lid of the Droste chocolate box strides a

little man with a walking stick. He has a conical hat on his head and a disc of plain chocolate for a body.

Ingmar rubs his eyes with his wrists, then looks out of the window.

The sky has begun to be distinguishable from the black meadow.

The little leaves on the branches of the weeping birch are still not visible, although the sun is just coming up over the treetops.

Spears of spring grass emerging through last year's carpet of dirty yellow, shaded by the house.

The alarm clock in the bedroom rings and is switched off. Käbi goes to pee, flushes the toilet and then comes out to the kitchen.

'Just think if I fell pregnant this time,' she says sleepily from behind him.

There is a suppressed smile in her voice. Her body still exudes the warmth of the bed.

'I'd forgotten you had to go to Västerås,' he says.

'Have you been awake long?'

'No.'

'I heard you at quarter to five.'

'Yes, I managed to pull the whole blessed shelf out of the fridge,' he says. 'Think the fixing's buggered again.'

'I'll take a look at it on Saturday,' she murmurs as she fills the enamel saucepan with water and puts it on the stove.

After a while there's a whistling between the two metal surfaces.

'Are you going out to Råsunda now – or were you thinking of doing something else?'

'I don't know,' he replies.

'Darling, take no notice of what they write in the newspapers,' she says. 'The only thing that matters is that everybody who was there loved the opera. I mean . . . if the entire audience gives a standing ovation. One that just goes on and on. Bravo Ingmar. Bravo.'

'I know – that's what counts.'

Through the window he sees Käbi getting into the taxi, then he kneels to plug the telephone back in, sits down with pounding heart and rings Lenn.

After the trumpet fanfares, a rigid curtain (with a curtain painted on it) is suddenly drawn up, revealing the scenery for a short prelude: it's springtime in Trulove's garden and a woman with an anxious face and a full beard is sitting in the arbour.

'Straight answers are what please me! Now I'm ready – one, two, three.'

A little man whose round body seems to be made of plain chocolate hurries in through a gap in the fence.

'Let's see, Putte, wait a bit. Let me find the word, it's a – hit!'

The members of the audience laugh, they breathe out, and the unexpected blast of air almost tips the unwieldy conical hat off the chocolate man's head. In that moment of genuine anxiety, Ragnar Ulfung's private face can be seen through the make-up before he recovers his composure.

'You're not lying? Please do say! Speak the truth to me today!'

The chocolate disc warbles a few sneering notes and points at the house with his walking stick; the door opens and onto the stage dances Ingmar's secretary Lenn in pale pink tights, with a patch of sweat showing between his buttocks.

'In our youth we think we're clever. I'm old Curt Berg, as daft as ever.'

The woman blushes and hides her face in her beard.

'My review contains no jeers – both the look and the sound deserve three cheers! Director Putte, don't look glum. These flowing tributes were justly won.'

His hand shaking, Ingmar replaces the receiver, wonders whether Lenn is lying to keep him happy, and can't make up his mind whether to unplug the phone again.

He ties the top of the rubbish bag, puts another in the bin under the sink and sees his mother come in. The bromural has left her dazed, and she trips over the sewing machine.

Ingmar doesn't know what to do; he follows a young man with red cheeks who is running to his room.

For a long while he just sits on the floor, his hands covering his face.

Then he tries to calm himself down by hunting out the old cinematograph and the battered purple tin with the words 'Frau Holle' on it.

But the little boy's fingerprints on the reflector mirror bring the young man out in a sweat.

He wants to hide the cinematograph again.

Remembers how breathless Father was when he opened the door, grabbed him by the hair and pulled him out of the wardrobe.

He still hadn't understood what he was accused of as he lay sprawled on the floor in front of his father. Blinking in the bright light, with his pyjama jacket all bunched up.

And presumably it was fear of his punishment that made him wet himself.

No, he wet himself in the second's relaxation before the sudden pain.

Or perhaps he was just dreadfully angry: shouting at his brother through the tears that he would kill him and not even noticing it had happened until Dag started to laugh.

He just stood there and let it happen.

And Dag ran and fetched his mother, the urine was wiped up, and only after Ingmar had been washed did she perform the humiliating ritual, while his father and big brother looked on.

The family had giggled as they turned him round

for inspection, made comments, laughed, and his father had dashed off to fetch the camera.

Allan Ekelund rings to congratulate him on the good reviews, *Dagens Nyheter, Svenska Dagbladet, Stockholms-Tidningen, Aftonbladet,* all the major papers. Ingmar thanks him quietly, changes the subject and asks his views on the new film instead.

'Can I count on your support?'

'I dare say you can do what you damn well please after all the fuss they made of *Virgin Spring.*'

'But what do *you* think?' asks Ingmar, hearing the hint of desperation in his own voice.

'Think? I'll need to read the script before I . . .'

'Of the idea, I mean.'

'I don't know.'

'Well I personally think, I'm convinced, that this film has got to be made, but I do realize it may sound rather dull to . . .'

Allan Ekelund laughs and agrees.

'But seriously,' says Ingmar. 'Do you think I'm being stupid, trying to force through this production?'

'Possibly.'

Ingmar walks across the wet paving stones in the garden at the back of the house, notes that the metal base of the sprinkler has left a rusty mark on the yellow brick under the coiled hose.

A white cat has jumped up onto the sill of the

music room window. She takes pleasure in balancing there. Seems to be looking in at Käbi's Bechstein grand, at the highly polished black of the lid.

Two clacking magpies chase each other round a birch, dive down to the waterlogged grass under the apple tree.

Ingmar takes a few steps, then stops in front of the grey-green tarpaulin covering the garden furniture.

He looks at the folds: dark accumulations of water and brown pine needles beneath dry, dusty alpine peaks.

Someone is burning wood and leaves. From one of the gardens along the road, an ash-grey column of smoke rises. It unbraids its way into a closed, white sky.

*   *   *

The daddy-long-legs vibrates in the glass jar, ticking and jerking, then flies round and lies still. The wood ant makes a new approach and the daddy-long-legs blunders off again. Dag laughs, his eyes scared. Ingmar tries to get closer, but is shoved out of the way by his big brother.

Is thrown onto the gravel and hits his back on the water butt behind the chapel of rest.

He gets to his feet and asks Käbi how the concert went.

There's a crackle on the line as she answers in

a rather distracted voice, 'Oh, it went quite well, actually.'

'That's good.'

'I shall be off to the Helanders' soon, but wait . . . Listen,' she says with barely suppressed delight.

'What am I supposed to . . .?'

He is interrupted by a sudden sound: a dry pop, several rapid clinks.

'Cheers, here's to you! The critics loved it.'

'You've bought champagne?' he asks.

'So should you have done.'

'I know,' he says, suddenly feeling his body slacken and relax.

'What are you going to do with your evening?'

'Have an early night, try to write a bit more,' he says with a big smile.

'Oh yes, how's it going for that poor priest of yours?'

'I don't know; I write far too slowly,' he answers. 'I've got to find the simple, everyday drama in it. The conflict between the human being and the profession of priest, in fact. Everyone thinks the subject sounds terribly boring.'

Ingmar laughs.

'But you seem to have started liking the priest a bit,' says Käbi.

'What else can I do? After all, I've only got him. To identify with, I mean. Last time I could divide myself between three of them. The boy, the doctor and the writer. But here, I'm shut inside the priest. And that's the whole idea, of course, my having nowhere to run to. Because that's how it would have been if I'd become a priest.'

Towards the left side of the etching, a woman with one bare breast is sitting on a chair. She is pointing in amusement at the hat lying on the floor. The orgy has entered its final stages; everyone is tired. The rod-like torches cast their punishing gleam. Beneath a broken mirror sits Ingmar, legs spread wide, frilled shirt open. His hair is unwashed and already a little too long. He decided not to shave this morning and stubble, pale grey and black, has developed. The yellow writing pad is on the table in front of him, among goblets and fruit.

Ingmar catches sight of the pencil in his right hand, its end chewed and frayed, its shiny paint cracked. His thumb and forefinger, pallid as pine, with complicated systems of intersecting ditches, riverbeds, the membrane of the cuticle over the pink base of the nail; yesterday's paper cut glints through a paler red.

He turns to a blank page and tells himself he can at least jot down the thoughts that occurred to him as he was working on the final phase of the opera production.

*

Ingmar is writing rapidly now, the pencil moves over the paper. The daddy-long-legs blunders into glass sides and metal lid. He tries to capture the central ideas, the plot, but tires of it, finds himself lingering increasingly over interiors, over scenes and dialogues and mood changes.

The teacher doesn't want to leave the priest's side, but he has no room for love inside him, Ingmar writes at the bottom of a page, and turns over quickly.

The priest feels he has no space within him to receive her, he continues, her need for affection and acknowledgment. So he has to steel himself, because of his inability.

Then she leaves him, once and for all, thinks Ingmar. Maybe that's the real nub of the story I'm going to tell. About a priest who can't bear God's silence, His lack of care. Unconscious of the fact that he's behaving the same way himself.

The teacher asks for love, but he turns away from her. He is nothing but a mute surface against her.

Against love.

So she leaves him in the end. Just as God has left him. And the priest is left alone, with his loneliness.

The pencil moves quickly again as Ingmar writes the teacher's words of love. Then comes the priest's sudden cruelty. He rejects her, but she doesn't go. She stays and accepts his malicious remarks. Cries, admits her own stupidity, but refuses to leave him. Realizing that she, too, has been selfish in her attitude to him, she says: Every time I felt hatred for you, I turned that hatred into compassion.

Surprised that the teacher has refused to leave the priest, Ingmar changes sides and writes that something may need to happen to force her to go.

She won't go of her own accord.

She's a terribly clingy, nauseating woman, he writes, but then crosses out the words with a lingering sense of having violated someone.

But after all, he tells himself, closing the yellow notepad, the idea is that the priest is left alone with God. Or the lack of God, if you like. Ingmar hunts through his previous workbook and finds an early entry in which he wrote that she (while she was still his wife) leaves him. In bitterness, he wrote.

That's the underlying assumption. Yet she refuses to give up once she's in place, thinks Ingmar as he goes closer to the glass jar standing by the brick wall, on the line between evening sun and sail-grey shadow. He kneels down and suddenly hears his mother speaking on the telephone behind the yellow windowpane in the vicarage.

'What a reception and what a first night! I could hardly believe it was you standing there on stage,' she says. 'My Putte, so celebrated.'

'What did Father think?'

'The King and Queen were there.'

The ticking, swiftly chirping movement in the jar has stopped.

'He didn't come,' Ingmar says quietly.

'You know what he's like – when he doesn't feel well enough to . . .'

'I just get so tired of it,' he interrupts.

The television is on in the background. Accompanying his mother's slow breathing. Ingmar senses her wish to backtrack, her tentative efforts, her awareness that he doesn't care if Agda went with her to the Opera House, if they saw Åkerhielm and old Mr Josephson in the stalls.

The daddy-long-legs is lying like a little blob of lead in the bottom of the jar, wingless, with just a few sticks for legs.

He can hear the Stjärnsund clock behind her as she lapses into silence, the soft swing of the pendulum.

'And congratulations on the prize . . . the Oscar,' she says hesitantly.

'Yes, I was pleased with that,' he mutters.

'I tried to ring, but then I realized you'd be busy with the premiere.'

Ingmar isn't conscious of leaving the front door open as he goes out. It's chilly in the garden. His shirt flaps in the wind, his vest is damp with sweat and cold against his back.

He runs down the drive. Strides past the car, the cherry tree and the plaited mass of rhododendron. Thinks his father can go to hell. Should be in an old people's home.

The white cat is scratching in the pile of sand and he aims a kick at her. She listlessly retreats a few metres and when he stamps his foot she glides round and vanishes under the fence.

Shivering, he walks on along the gravelled road, catches a faint smell of smoke and reflects that he must have been quite happy when he used to creep in and play the little organ in the darkness under the stairs.

But the notes died abruptly, in a gasp. He moved aside, having heard footsteps in the gravel.

Crunching.

He breaks into a run again, past the row of detached houses. Has got to check the bonfire's been put out properly for the night. He looks in on the level plots of garden and repeats to himself that even one tiny spark left alight could quickly flare up.

A dog barks from behind a door.

Ingmar steps over a low fence, undeterred by the light shining from the upstairs windows of the house, walks round to the back but can see no trace of anything burning. He goes on over another fence to the garden beyond, breaks into a run as he smells smoke but finds no fire.

Through a narrow gap in a fir hedge, he stumbles

35

out onto a lawn, past a steel frame with a red plastic swing, and across a gravel path. On the far side of the big house he can see the ground is glowing, a flickering display of darkness. Breathlessly he hurries to the spot and starts to stamp. Black dust whirls about his legs, glowing barques rise into the air, winking. He can feel the heat from the ground, the burning sensation round his calves, but carries on stamping until he notices the figure on the outer edge of the circle of light.

A slim head at hip height. The wet gleam in its big eyes.

'I saw the fire,' said Ingmar. 'Thought I ought to lend a hand.'

'Ah, but I'm happy to let it carry on burning for a while.'

Ingmar can't make out her face. The faint gleam illuminates the side of her body, the back of her neck. A dented extension of the night; she seems to be sitting on an upturned wheelbarrow. A slim leg glints, motionless.

'I live a few houses along.'

'I know,' she says with amusement in her voice.

'I saw the smoke earlier.'

'Is Käbi abroad?'

'No, in Västerås.'

The lips are moistened by a coarse tongue.

'And you thought it would be all right to pay a visit – if Jan-Carl wasn't at home.'

'No,' whispers Ingmar, looking at the pool of sparkling light, seeing the darkness force its way up through the faint glow.

'You just wanted to check that I put the fire out properly?'

3

Taking care not to damage the emulsion, he thrusts the strip of film into a glass jar. His father's multiple faces spring loose, hundreds of identical pictures fill the void.

He screws the lid back on again and puts the jar on the passenger seat beside him.

Slowly they approach the flaking, white, medieval church, as air-green fields run by on the right-hand side.

'I can drop the two of you at the gate,' says Ingmar.

'What for?' asks his father.

'So you don't have to walk up the hill.'

'I can walk.'

A low, loose wall of unhewn granite runs round the churchyard and the towerless, elongated church with arched windows. Streaks of pink run across walls coated in crumbling plaster. Through swaying, leafy crowns there are glimpses of a steep roof with cracked tiles.

Ingmar wonders whether to leave the film script in the car. Lenn has typed up the first draft. Twenty-five pages in a pallid cardboard folder. Ingmar has planned to ask his father if he would like to read it.

*

Erik rests, one hand against the wall, his cuff wrink-
ling the mottled skin on the back of his hand.

'Are you in pain?' Karin asks him quietly.

He doesn't reply, just stands there, waiting.

The strained sound of the summoning begins, the
great bell sighs and Karin looks up to the red-painted
bell-tower on the hill behind the church.

Ingmar scratches his head through his cap and starts
telling his father about the film he's going to make,
about the priest who realizes he's lost his faith. Who
feels he's just going through the motions of priesthood.

His father jingles the coins in the pocket of his
light-coloured coat and screws up his eyes as he looks
at the sealed whiteness of the sky.

'So that's sort of why,' says Ingmar. 'Why I wanted
to come to an ordinary church.'

'Ordinary?' mumbles his father.

'Somewhere that wasn't the Royal Chapel and . . .'

'There's no difference,' Erik interrupts, and starts
walking.

Ingmar follows, keeping pace with him.

'I've brought the script with me, actually. A first
draft. It's no masterpiece, but . . .'

He falters, trying to read that scroll of silent faces,
as small as the fingerprints on the glass jar. His father
varies in brightness, depending on changing angles
and degrees of transparency. But the coiled, twisted
ribbon of pictures shows him nothing but repetition.

* * *

In a dark oil painting, Jesus hangs on his crosspiece. Six perfect jets of blood spurt from the wound in his side in thin arcs, straight down onto the heads of six men.

Ingmar stands in the narrow pew while his parents sit down.

His gaze travels from the brass chandelier up to the balcony with the pointed arch and the old organ. There is movement behind the balcony rail, the organist. A woman wearing a black blouse under a pale grey or blue cardigan. He happens to meet her eyes and turns away. Knocks a hymn book onto the floor, leaves it there, wipes a trembling hand across his mouth. He can't make sense of what he has seen. A woman of about fifty, with arched, plucked eyebrows, lips in a tight line and deep wrinkles round the downturned corners of her mouth.

Then the organ bellows give a huff and the first notes squeeze their way up through the pipework.

He remembers the beautiful, straight nose, the hair speckled with grey; he hunts through his memory, searches back past all Käbi's friends.

It sounds as though the organist is deliberately playing it wrong, with strange changes of register. Erik looks as if he is about to make a protest, but stays silent.

The middle-aged priest with hair down over his ears runs his thin hands over his chasuble.

Green velvet embroidered with silver.

He coughs, explains that he's sick and intends to hold only a short service.

The priest looks at his watch and then gestures hesitantly to the congregation.

'But what's this?' mutters Erik, gripping the back of the pew in front of him.

'You could take over,' Ingmar whispers to him with a flutter of anticipation in his stomach.

He turns round and sees the organist standing there, her big body leaning against the balcony rail. The very thought of trying to avoid her gaze draws his eyes upward. She stares straight at him and puts out her pale tongue.

His guts churn, he begins to remember and sits down in the pew, although the congregation is getting to its feet.

That's not right, he thinks.

A grey woman is faintly visible through a poor combination of optometric lenses. Every new polishing of the lenses makes the picture more distorted; it comes into focus but shrinks or narrows.

A white crocheted bedcover, broad hips. A hand is thrown out, the flesh of the arm quivers. The crocheted pattern on the naked skin.

The clarity of the picture improves in jerky stages as the woman turns away and pulls open a kitchen drawer.

She blurs, then comes into sharp focus again.

Curved round the outer edge of the lens, she approaches him with a paring knife in her left hand and starts to laugh as she says she's going to cut off his backside.

Now she's sitting with her back to his back, her hands resting on the organ keyboard, Ingmar thinks.

The inscrutable face, the red-dyed hair.

He doesn't know how many times he slept with her.

After rehearsals.

Strindberg's *The Pelican* at the Student Theatre in Stockholm.

Swanwhite.

And then he left her, fled up to Våroms. She wasn't right in the head, he told himself.

Even back then he was increasingly aware of imitating his father's calculated punishments. He has no need to look at the moon-shaped scars on his knuckles to remember that singsong note of hysteria and relief.

Her face against the bathroom floor, the way she dried her tears and began licking between his toes.

He resists his own fantasy, tells himself it will stay shut inside his head, it is unreal; thinks she won't really go so far as to sabotage the hymn. But at that moment she rises on the balcony behind him, the organ like a giant carapace on her back, and shouts out over the congregation that Ingmar Bergman used to promise this and promise that and fuck her like a little poodle.

The priest just stands there, not seeing his flock. His thin, bearded face is hanging directly over the bloated angel – with carefully arranged golden hair and squinting, red-rimmed eyes – on the pulpit.

Ingmar wonders if the priest is nervous because he has realized Erik Bergman is sitting in the pew in front of him.

'This is my beloved son,' he says weakly, and then stops.

God sits with his crown and full, curly beard, his son on his knee, squeezed between his thighs, hanging on the cross. They are in the middle of the screen on the high altar, in the middle of the choir. Surrounded by ten smaller altarpieces: John the Baptist, Mary and the baby Jesus, Birgitta with her book, Evangelists and others.

Ingmar starts walking down to the car park, turns and sees that his father has stopped on the gravel outside the church door.

Red spots flare on his pale cheeks.

Erik is looking out over the fields to the rain-burdened sky and breathing through half-open mouth.

Ingmar turns back and says he can fetch his father's stick from the car, in an attempt to get him to come straight away.

He is afraid the organist will come out and speak to them.

The priest scratches his beard, mumbles something about being honoured to welcome such a visitor, and Ingmar's father tries to catch his eye as he comes towards them across the gravel.

'I loved *The Seventh Seal*,' the priest smiles, holding out his hand to Ingmar.

'Did you,' says Ingmar very quietly.

'Must have seen it ten times.'

'This is my father, Erik Bergman.'

'Pleased to meet you,' says the priest.

'Pastor to the royal family,' explains Ingmar.

They shake hands and Ingmar peers into the dark porch. Sees a figure at the bottom of the stairs, a rounded shape against the shiny curve of the landing.

'We must go,' mumbles Erik.

'But what about the coffee?' says the priest, trying to steer Ingmar towards a gap in the churchyard wall. 'My wife.' He indicates the vicarage over the crown of the hill, beyond the bell-tower.

* * *

Erik leans heavily against the arched front wing. They have stopped at the edge of the road, only ten kilometres or so south of Sigtuna. Beside them a meadow, anchored there by a glacial boulder. With the blue edge of the forest in one direction, a ditch and then fields of rape in the other.

Corn mint and shady horsetail brush the car tyres.

The slight articulation of the grass stalks from node to node, the broader blades and meagre ears.

Motionless, awash with insects.

Karin unscrews the top of the thermos flask and pours the coffee.

'Did he recognize you?' she asks.

'Oh yes, I think so,' Erik replies.

'I was almost hoping you would take the priest by the ear and show him how things are done, Father,' says Ingmar, and can hear how ingratiating he sounds.

'Like when Bishop Giertz was due to preach at the Palace,' says his mother. 'The chapel was full, the Queen was in her seat, but no Bishop. After fifteen minutes Father got up, went to the front and said he would take the service.'

And the Queen clapped, Dag told him one Sunday. But she stopped when the King gave her a look. Her cheeks flushed and she started scratching herself, down there.

Like lead-grey cloth, velvet perhaps. With a pattern of white circles round black pearls. Then the little butter-fly opens its blue wings and whirls away.

Ingmar's father straightens up; his light-coloured coat pulls tight across his tensed shoulders.

His narrow tie, his crumpled waistcoat.

Pale top lip and thin white moustache.

His nostrils are flared, but his eyes are candied with an elusive calm.

'No cake or biscuits?' asks Erik and blows on his coffee.

'You told me not to bring any,' answers Karin.

'I'm only asking,' he mumbles.

Ingmar's mother fingers the necklace hanging against the front of her blouse and says they could actually sit on the grass, as it's dry.

His father does not even bother to answer.

His thin hair is ruffled up from his shiny scalp by the breeze.

Ingmar fetches chocolate from the car and his father tries some, drinks his coffee and sucks his cheeks in a little.

'This is proper chocolate,' he says.

'From Holland,' says Ingmar. 'It's called Droste.'

'Why don't we have Droste?'

'I don't know,' says Karin, looking amused.

A row of blue and red oil cans is lined up at the edge of the forest. And over the treetops, a single-engine plane glides soundlessly.

'What a strange service,' says Ingmar's mother.

'Strange? It was shortened,' replies his father, shaking the drips out of his coffee mug. 'But I expect that suited Putte,' he says, flashing Ingmar an affectionate, teasing look. 'Do you know,' he says. 'You were only three the first time you went to church.'

Ingmar tries to hold back a smile.

'It was Christmas Eve and I pulled you on my green sledge through the snowdrifts, past the Works.'

His mother looks at the ground, as if suddenly gripped by a terrible premonition, but then she merely looks embarrassed.

His father tells the story of the little voice he suddenly heard from the congregation during his sermon: 'I think that's quite enough from Father.'

Ingmar gives a naked laugh, surprising himself.

His mother's left hand pats the air above her hair.

Ingmar opens the car door and helps his father in, then retrieves the film script from the front seat and says it would be nice to hear what he thinks of it.

'Is that so?' Erik sighs, putting the folder on his lap.

Ingmar slams the car door shut, rests his hand on the roof, feels the heat of the black metal and looks out over the rape field, observing the angle of its yellow square against the plane of white sky, the way the space narrows near the horizon until the white finally pastes itself to the yellow.

He brakes carefully and stops outside the entrance of number 19, Storgatan. The bushes in front of the building tremble in the wind. A soggy mitten is wedged under the low fence.

'So that was the first church,' he explains, looking

at his father's face in the rear-view mirror. 'I thought maybe five more, if the two of you would like to come.'

'I haven't got time,' his father says to his mother.

A smooth, copper-coloured shadow is cast over Ingmar. As if through brown glass, covering him like a coat. He squeezes his eyes tight shut and grits his teeth. How stupid can you be, he thinks, and decides to go to bed hungry to punish himself.

Sitting behind the steering wheel again later, he shuts his eyes and views the brief farewell from a great height. Interlocking rectangles of house roofs. Black tin, red tin, red tile. Terraces with racks for beating carpets. Chimney pots, guttering. And between the houses, Storgatan in afternoon light. The car gleams like a drop of tar on a zinc sill. Ingmar offers his father the rest of the chocolate. His father declines, but does nothing to stop Ingmar slipping the box into his coat pocket.

The strip of film in the jar has doubled back on itself, is even fourfold in places. Sometimes matching up, simply looking fleshier, but sometimes creating distorting displacements, grotesqueries.

* * *

Ingmar hangs his keys on the hook, puts the jar on the hat rack, enters the yellow glow and treads awkwardly on a high-heeled shoe. The pale grey coat is lying on the linoleum in the hall. A plastic bag in which he can dimly make out some bread, ham and a box of eggs.

'I told Käbi I'd be staying in town,' he mutters, 'because I needed to be on my own for a while.'

She raises her head from the pillow.

'Maimu's visiting,' he explains. 'And they're more than happy to do without me.'

She sighs and turns away.

'The thing is . . . I don't think it would bother Käbi,' he says without looking at her. 'She was living in an open relationship when she met me and . . .'

He unbuttons his shirt and someone starts to laugh, out on the stairs.

'The only thing she's said,' he goes on, 'is that she wants to know the truth, which I choose to view as a lie.'

Outside the window, a woman's voice shouts something and a car door shuts.

'Yes,' he says, prodding his own stomach.

These retakes, less and less recognizable. The sherry glasses on the table. And the very banality of the situation. The evening light coming through dirty windows; his trousers over the back of the chair; the springiness of the side of the bed; the sound of a sock on a rough heel.

'What shall we do?' he asks, his eye following the pale pink inner curve of her thigh towards her groin.

Her face is averted, her neck tense. A flimsy sheet

corner covers the middle of her body, moulds itself to the expectant rise and fall of her belly, slips over the blunted chalk tip of her nipple.

'What do you say?' he asks. 'Shall we be unfaithful now?'

'Maybe.'

'That's why we're here, isn't it?' he says, and sees her nod.

From one branch of the chandelier hangs her skin-coloured bra. He has only just noticed it. Presumably the idea was that it would make him laugh when he came in. The shoes in the hall, the coat on the floor, the slacks, and so on.

She moves closer, cuddles up in his arms, and he starts telling her he is going to visit some Uppland churches with his father.

Ready for the new film.

But he would really like to admit that it was only one church and that his father has refused to come to any more.

'And this evening he's going to read the first draft of the script,' says Ingmar, and hears someone stop outside the door of the flat, just as he puts his hand on her thigh.

'Oops,' she says indistinctly, with a smile.

'We'll do as we like,' he whispers.

'Will we?'

'But our lives will be simpler if we decide not to sleep with each other, of course.'

'Then I think we should eat what I brought for breakfast, instead.'

'Except I wasn't going to eat anything this evening,' he says.

'Aren't you hungry?'

He gets up from the bed and goes over to the window. Along the summer-bleached street swirl vast numbers of seeds from the elm trees. A drift of brittle little saucers is lifted by the wind. Eddies round the legs of a man in black with a poodle on a lead.

'In the film, the complication arises when the priest admits his inability to feel love,' he says. 'Because it happens at the very moment the teacher realizes she has no choice: her task is to love him. I've thought about her a lot, I mean . . . Is there anything more pathetic than pleading for love?'

When she doesn't answer, he turns round; she has fallen asleep, her mouth open, and he feels nothing but relief at the absence of infidelity.

Swift wingbeats, a mouth moistened.

There's a sound from behind the linen cupboard, not like a whisper, more like a sheet of paper plastered against the wall, vibrating as the air moves when someone opens the front door.

He puts his shoulder to one back corner of the heavy piece of furniture, moves it out a little way and sees that the wall itself is bulging.

Bulging out and sinking back in again, as if slowly breathing.

And when he touches the wall, there is no solidity to it. He applies pressure and his hand goes right through the wallpaper.

They tried to hide a hole, he thinks. Covered it over to conceal the space behind.

Ingmar rips down a big strip of wallpaper, feels round the edge with his fingers and tries to see what is there.

He carefully works his head in between the cupboard and the crumbling brick wall, and looks into a little flat earmarked for demolition, with yellowing newspaper covering the windows.

Against the inner wall, under the black gas meter, sits a stocky woman with an earnest, childish face.

There are crutches lying on the dirty floor in front of her.

Hair plaited for the night, colourless as rope, rests against a large bosom.

A wet-nurse, thinks Ingmar, glimpses her breath against the grey brick of the chimneybreast and wonders if she is feeling the cold.

'Though it warms me up inside,' she whispers, lowering her eyes, 'every time a child takes its life.'

'What did you say?'

'Sorry,' she mumbles, her cheeks and neck flushing. 'But don't you remember us meeting up in Dalarna? By the rushing filmy surface of the wide river? I didn't push you, but I think I lied to you, didn't tell you about the pain in your lungs and the way the sky goes all black and shaky, as if it's behind a frosted window, before it . . .'

4

Lighter than the night-bright sky, the sea lies there. Moves as sluggishly as oil, in a scarcely perceptible swell.

While the Landsort lighthouse appears as a column of warm air.

The beach is still dark, the stunted pines hidden.

Ingmar realizes he should have taken Valium two hours ago. Now it's too near morning. He has already heard Käbi mumble something from the bed.

He strikes out sentence after sentence, as the priest reveals his doubts to the teacher in the vestry.

He finds it difficult to talk about, thinks Ingmar, wondering how he would have accommodated his own lack of faith if he had become a priest.

He experimentally presses his finger harder against the edge of the little envelope containing a razor blade.

Perhaps it's the same for everyone.

At this moment he finds it hard to recall if his father used to talk about his own faith, if he ever put any of his questions about God into words at all.

The only thing Ingmar can bring to mind is a poem, written to his mother in 1912.

He crosses out the superficial words that liken communion to cannibalism. And then the rest of the unfocused dialogue.

What he really likes about the scene is that the teacher listens to the priest like a child, happy to have the opportunity to respond 'I understand' without being contradicted.

But the priest can't see her.

Just like Peer Gynt, Don Juan and Rakewell, he will be described throughout the film as a difficult, disagreeable person. Because the audience always retains the essential capacity for reconciliation, thinks Ingmar. Even as he is making them feel that the teacher should give up on the priest, that she is demeaning herself, that he will never give her what she needs.

The summer morning seems to brighten out of the pale night as Käbi stands in the bedroom door.

'Too hot to sleep,' she says drowsily.

'There isn't a breath of wind.'

He can't see her; her face is featureless and wreathed in shadow.

'How's it going?'

'Fairly well, actually.'

'I'm glad.'

In the window stands an ornament, a pink china pig, with a hole in its back for a candle.

'I was just reading through the conversation with the fisherman,' he says. 'Do you remember when we went up to Boda to visit the clergyman who married us – and we thought everyone seemed a bit strange?'

'Yes, that's right. Someone had committed suicide.'

'He'd often gone there to talk things over with the priest, but then he just did it,' says Ingmar with a smile, noticing a dead fly in the hole in the pig's back. 'My guess is, Father will say I ought to cut the scenes about . . .'

'But he won't read it, you know,' she interjects. 'I don't suppose he's even looked at the first draft.'

'No, but then I told Mother he needn't bother with that, I rang to tell her when I was getting near the end of the new draft.'

'Oh, I see,' she mumbles.

'What?'

'Just that . . . you can't really afford to delay handing out the script to the actors and . . .'

'I know,' he answers.

Something quivers in the window and Ingmar looks out. He takes a while to realize the movement is coming from the china pig, a glittering of its snout. He bends forward and sees that its red lips have got wet; there are drops in the dust on the windowsill.

'I thought I'd dreamt it,' says Käbi without trying to meet his eye. 'But yesterday, after I'd taken my tablet and fallen asleep, the phone rang. Can you guess who it was? Gun. She sounded drunk. Wanted to talk to me, she said. I know I should have hung up, but I didn't . . .'

'What did she want?' he asks tersely.

'She said you never ever tell the truth.'

'That's a lie.'

'There were other things she wanted to tell me, too,' mumbles Käbi, and leaves the room.

Ingmar reads the part of the script where the priest visits the scene of the suicide, and writes in the margin that he can only see the fisherman's body from a distance, already transformed into a pile of earth on the ground in front of the priest and the others.

And they are standing there talking, he realizes, even though there is no dialogue for the scene yet.

He can't hear them.

It must be to do with the distance. Or the roar of the water against the rocks.

Perhaps it will stay that way.

Because the distance and the lack of voices heightens the sense of God's silence. And how small and trivial a dead body seems.

Momentarily, his thoughts stray via the brick chapel in the Sophia Hospital to the Chapel of Rest, the sun shining through the opalescent glass in the little windows, and then to a huge viper.

On Tuesday he had gone down to the beach after breakfast.

The polished stones on the beach, just before it banked steeply down to the shoreline, were dazzling in the sun.

Ingmar knows he recalled the glint in his father's nostrils long ago as he stood with the sharp spade poised above his elder brother's chest and neck.

Still agitated.

And he was wrapped in those memories as he discovered the viper warming itself in the sun.

The muted gleam of the thick body.

Presumably it was the surprise that caused his panic, he thinks. Made him feel under attack.

Ingmar wondered if the snake was sick as he took the last quick steps, his heart pounding and his arms raised, holding the heavy stone unsteadily above his head.

A sudden thwack and a rattling echo among the pebbles.

As soon as the snake stopped quivering he went up to it. Rolled the stone away from its crushed head with his foot. Backed off and left it lying there. Told himself that a buzzard or a flock of seagulls would take it. That there might well be mink and foxes on Torö.

From the paved terrace facing the sea, the veranda door opens into a small dining room, its interior weighed down by a hired grand piano. From the piano corner, a pale pink rag rug struggles over the vinyl floor and in under a table by a naked window. Above the window, the bracket for the curtain rail hangs loose on one side, while on the other there are just screw holes in the wall.

Through the scratched, orange plexiglass shade of the ceiling light, the dim outlines of the kitchen can be seen: the stove, the draining board with a packet of biscuits on it, and some oxe-eye daisies in a bottle.

To the left, through the half-open door, the corner of one bed is visible. The heavy, crocheted bedspread in the gloom of the closed roller blinds.

The watery morning light finding its way in through the door from the nursery roves around in time to Ingmar's quick voice: 'No, what? We don't get a newspaper out here.'

The telephone flex stretches taut over his chest as he turns to the window to see if Käbi is still lying in the hammock.

'They bricked up every single gap,' his mother tells him. 'Every window, every . . .'

'Can they really do that?' he says.

'All they'll say is that there wasn't any formal decision; it happened spontaneously.'

'Oh well, that's all right then!'

'Perhaps things will quieten down a bit in Berlin now,' says Karin.

'Quieten down? What do you m . . .?'

His father's voice can be heard in the distance. Like in a cake tin, he thinks.

'We're just on our way out,' his mother says.

'Yes I've got to go, too,' Ingmar replies, sitting down on the guest bed. 'But can I . . . I was just wondering if Father has had time to read it yet.'

'Read what?'

'My film script, the one I sent.'

'Er, I don't know – shall I . . .'

'But hasn't he said anything about it?' Ingmar interrupts.

'Shall I fetch him?'

'There's no need,' says Ingmar, and chews his thumbnail.

The ground is covered in gingery pine needles and has a scent of warmth. Käbi is lying in the grubby hammock. Almost invisible, encased in its taut sides.

'Had he read any of it?' she asks drowsily. 'Though I expect you only spoke to Karin.'

'Father was out for a walk. But he seems to have found it quite moving. When the priest is trying to comfort Mrs Persson and asks if he can pray with her. You know, she just shakes her head and says no.'

'That's a good scene,' she replies evasively.

'Yes.'

He runs his hand along the hard curve of her backside and spine. Swings her heavy body through the shadowy netting. Aware that she has not allowed herself to be deceived.

'You realize, don't you, that you can't hang around waiting much longer?' she says.

'It's not that I need his approval. It's not that. I'm just trying to let him share a bit of it, or somehow . . .'

'Do whatever you like,' she says impatiently.

The fixings of the hammock creak a little. Wood ants are climbing down the tree trunk.

'Käbi, it really isn't my fault you spoke to Gun on the phone,' he says. 'So there's no need to be angry with me about it.'

'Why should I be angry?'

'You'll have to answer that yourself,' he says.

'Angry's the wrong word, but you know when Maimu spent the night here and you stayed in town?' says Käbi. 'That night, on impulse . . . I got up, got dressed, took her car and drove to your work flat.'

'Oh.'

'Is there anything you want to tell me?' she asks.

'No.'

'The door to the flat wasn't locked, Ingmar,' she says, trying to smile. 'You'd forgotten to lock the front door.'

His heart is beating fast, he bites his thumbnail, tries to think clearly, but can see only his own stupid face as he tells an older boy Nitti is a whore. He is constantly aware of simply repeating the lies Dag has spread about him, lies about all the filthy things he likes and can be persuaded to do, yet he can't stop himself.

'It must have been about two in the morning.'

'What are you trying to say, Käbi?'

'We're trying for a baby, yet you . . .'

'I know,' he interrupts.

'Ingmar, I recognize a guilty conscience when I see one. What's all this about? You don't even know. You hope that I'll be taken in, don't you? That it's just a game; that I didn't go into the flat.'

Ingmar shuts the boot of the car, sets off on foot through nettles and fireweed. Goes on down the slope towards the water. Feels the slopping weight in the can, the tug of the stiff handle.

Tiny connections glitter in the dry grass. Threads, spiderwork. The petrol sloshes softly in its can, the silky tops of grasses graze the metal.

On the beach he sets down the can, puts on the gardening gloves, approaches the snake and holds his breath as he lifts the body, which has gone stiff in the sun and stuck to the ground beneath.

The black blood.

Bits of shingle drop off and scatter as he drags it away from the clump of reeds, to the part of the beach out of sight of the house.

He shakes the gloves off, letting them fall, and unscrews the lid of the can.

Pours some petrol, then some more, wipes his hands on his trousers, fishes out the box of matches and strikes one.

The flames blaze up, then gently incline one way. Seem to be seeking him out. He moves the can away and stands watching as the snake slowly darkens and shrivels.

When the process is almost complete, he picks up the gloves and throws them onto the fire.

Then he gets to his knees, crawls across and builds a little cairn over the remains.

He stands up, moves away and suddenly smiles to himself, takes the can and looks at the small mound of stones again before he walks off.

When he sees the hammock swaying empty between the two trees, a sudden anxiety sighs within him, like a gas flame. So rapidly that it must have been there already, half hidden in lost memory, colourless. Now it mixes with his more rapid steps, roaming, jolting, scanning with his more frightened eyes.

Ingmar has to stop himself from shouting out as he goes into the house, searches through the rooms, behind doors, the kitchen, the cleaning cupboard, the guest bed in the nursery, the toilet, the shower curtain.

He comes to a stop in the darkness of the bedroom. Senses the momentum of his body turning. Wipes his mouth with his hand and takes one weak step back.

The sunlight is pressing on the dusty window. And the rectangle forms an over-exposed, pornographic picture.

A bleached little photo, with no immediate definition.

Käbi is lying naked on a sunlounger, eyes closed. Her black hair in heavy, twisting strands, her neck and shoulders, her sturdy arms resting at her sides, the flattened weight of her breasts, almost obscured by a reflection, the slightly swollen stomach with the vertical caesarian scar, the dark shape of her pubic hair, her long legs, slightly parted towards the sea, her feet and toes.

Ingmar goes out onto the terrace and sits down on a garden chair without looking at her. Even so, he notes that she is rolling over onto her stomach, her sunhat is in motion and settles on her head.

'What's this? What are you trying to prove?'

'I'm sunbathing,' she replies calmly. 'But of course I can put some clothes on if you want.'

'No, don't do that.'

She fixes him with a look, trying to sound light-hearted.

'Ingmar? There's not a soul here.'

'So why are you lying there like that, displaying yourself?'

'Just leave it,' she says, and sits up, pulling her knees under her and wrapping her arms round them.

'What are you hoping to . . .?'

'Can you leave me in peace now?' she snaps.

He gets up from the chair, walks through the house, slams the door behind him, feels the smarting pain just below his knee but carries on across the stepping stones in the front garden and climbs into the car, turns the key in the ignition, gets into gear, presses the accelerator and brings the clutch pedal up so sharply that the wheels spin, spraying gravel.

He turns out into the road and drives past all the signs he and Lenn, laughing, had painted: No Entry, Beware of the Dog, Beware of Big, Ugly Apes and so on.

* * *

Ingmar stands at the window contemplating the bumpy tarmac road past the casemates and the vast oak outside the gates of the film studios.

Behind him, Lenn pushes in the Danish plywood chair, deposits the post that has arrived since last Thursday on the table, returns to his typewriter and says he had a call from a journalist the day before yesterday.

'Oh yes, who was it?'

'Well maybe we needn't name any names, but . . .'

Lenn's voice tails off as he lines up a sheet of paper with the roller.

'What did he want this time?'

'He'd heard,' says Lenn slowly, winding the paper into the machine, 'that Svensk Filmindustri is planning to produce the most boring film in the history of Swedish cinema, and he said he's writing an article about how these things get decided.'

'Who the hell is going round talking crap about my film?' asks Ingmar, wishing he could go to sleep.

His face is tired after all that squinting at the summer day.

The leaves shifting between shadowy soft and blindingly bright.

He shuts his eyes and starts thinking about holidays at Våroms. Remembers that his father could never stand the sunlight there. Remembers how he maintained it was merciless, and hung thick blankets over the roller blinds. Lay in bed with his eyes closed.

'Shouldn't Mother be here?'

Ingmar realizes he is standing on the balcony of their summer house, under the roof with the funny wooden arch, leaning on the balustrade with his eyes shut.

In his nostrils is the smell of the warm gravel far below.

The screaming sensation in his stomach.

Sees the silvery circle of grass stand itself on end in the liquid darkness.

And hears Teddy's agitated bark and his big brother's voice repeating something behind his back, baiting and mocking.

But Dag had no idea how easy it would have been for me to jump, thinks Ingmar.

He opens his eyes: reflected in the window that looks onto the shaded façade of the studio's technical department, an ungainly body slides into the office.

'Bengt,' mumbles Ingmar, without turning round.

'You've got *The Pleasure Garden* this year,' he wheezes. 'And I don't suppose you've even finished *Through a Glass Darkly.*'

'What do you mean?'

'The scripts for *The Pleasure Garden*, and this *Painting on Wood* of yours. More Strindberg plays for the radio, *The Seagull* in Malmö, *The Rake's Progress* at the Opera House. What I mean is, who needs a Bergman film about a doubting priest?'

'Not many people.'

'I've taken soundings from the Board; it's a lot of money and nobody's really interested in this production.'

'Dymling thinks . . .'

'And I shall be doing my best to get it stopped.'

'At least you're being honest.'

Ingmar is oblivious to which book it is he takes from the shelf and tears in two. He throws it down, takes another, rips it apart and throws it against the wall, takes another and hurls it across the room, sweeps a whole row of books to the floor.

Still out of breath, he goes over to his desk and dials Dymling's number. Feels his hands shaking and the sweat prickling the back of his neck.

'Were you asleep?'

'What? Asleep, not bloody likely.'

Ingmar talks quickly, tells Dymling there's a

conspiracy against his production. Somebody leaking to the press that it's the most boring film of all time.

'Yes, I heard the grumbling had started,' drawls Dymling.

'Why just now? After all, *Virgin Spring* did pretty well, and . . .'

'But where the hell's the script, eh? Without a script . . .'

He coughs as Ingmar assures him it's finished. It just needs duplicating, he explains. His father has already read it three times.

'It's ready – you'll have it tomorrow.'

'But maybe it would be wiser to postpone making the film,' Dymling says.

It all began with him putting the tin soldiers and animals in various glass jars with lids. Allowing the light to be refracted, captured and made to cast shadows. Of course he didn't really believe they were talking.

Ingmar is sitting alone at the little editing table with four spool winders. His foot rests on the pedal. The reflection runs across his face. Nothing can be heard but the electrical whirr, the panting rotation of the spools and the whisper of the strip of film.

Then there's the sound of squeaky voices. A conversation ends and a man with an ungainly body leaves the room.

In the monitor, the picture is projected onto a flat

surface. Ingmar sees himself throwing books onto a floor with abrupt movements.

He fast forwards past that section and then slows the spool:

'There was no need to tidy up specially for us,' says Börje Lundh in a strange, deep voice, floating light-footed through the scattered, ripped books.

For some reason he has a pair of scissors in his hand and Gunnar is sporting a silly little parting in his hair and joking that he wants it that way.

'Feels good,' he says.

'For you, maybe,' answers Ingmar with a smile. 'But think of us, of all the people obliged to look at your side parting all autumn.'

'Well, perhaps a Kennedy quiff would look better,' jokes Börje.

'I think I'll stick with the parting,' says Gunnar.

Börje runs his fingers through Gunnar's hair and holds the yellow ends between finger and thumb.

'Is this from *The Pleasure Garden*?'

'We've got to try to think,' says Ingmar. 'How does this priest's life look? I mean, he hasn't got anybody any more to tell him what to wear or how to do his hair.'

'So what does he do?'

'Buys the same clothes as always, and drags himself off to the barber's in Frostnäs when he absolutely has to.'

There's a ripple of laughter.

'He hasn't really changed his hairstyle since he was at school,' Ingmar goes on. 'And it gives me no pleasure to say it, but that brings us straight back to your stupid parting, Gunnar.'

'A schoolboy,' titters Börje.

'Who happens to have got a little older,' says Ingmar. 'Which we must try to convey by the haircut.'

'Who needs actors when there are hairdressers?' mutters Gunnar.

'But it's no good all flattened like this,' continues Ingmar.

'Is my hair flattened?'

'And it mustn't stick out all over the place, either.'

Gunnar laughs.

Börje opens the door and says he can do a cut that hints at an old style beneath hair that's just been left to grow, so it looks as if was a long time since the priest last went to the barber's in Frostnäs.

Ingmar goes into the pink room they use when the canteen is busy. P.A. blows out his cheeks and Sven laughs, his face averted.

'Sometimes you think of all the tricks you've learnt: stylish spotlighting and hair filmed against the light, all those carefully arranged foregrounds, perspectives and . . .'

'Then I come along and say I want it without shadows,' says Ingmar. 'Like a perfectly ordinary November day.'

'And I love you for it,' replies Sven, flushing round his blond eyebrows and starting to leaf through the folder of photos of Torsång church.

'It's superb,' says Ingmar after a while.

'Isn't it just?' responds P.A. 'We'll be able to copy it almost exactly.'

'Though I'd like it a bit narrower.'

'Then we'll make it a touch longer.'

'What's it going to cost, do you reckon?'

'Hard to say.'

'Good job greaseproof paper's still cheap, Sven.'

'But I'd like a roof on the church, so we don't start cutting corners if we find we're running out of time.'

'Don't look at me,' says P.A.

'Will it be expensive?' asks Ingmar.

'Not as expensive as the floor,' says Sven with a big smile.

'Why, what about the floor?'

'Don't look at me,' says Sven.

P.A. turns his stiff body towards Ingmar:

'The thing is, I talked to Lennart, and we wondered, I mean, wouldn't it be great to put down a proper stone floor? It'll cost us, of course, but think of the acoustics.'

On the screen, Ingmar sees himself in miniature: he gets up, turns off the light on the editing table and leaves the room, comes back for his jacket and goes out again.

*

Then he stops the film, looks at the faint picture on the dull surface, winds back a little way and gets to his feet. He can feel the warmth from the metal shade closing round his hand like water as he switches off the lamp on the editing table.

Out in the corridor he feels for his keys and realizes he has left them in his jacket, turns and opens the door again, walks through a shadow the size of himself and takes the garment from the back of the chair, dragging the chair with him a little way, before leaving the editing room.

5

A flowery cushion tucked behind her neck, Käbi sits curled up in the armchair with the duplicated script on her knee. A nutty smell of spirits rises from the flimsy pages.

Ingmar is holding a cupped hand under his chin as he stands at the window, eating biscuits.

'Is the priest still you?'

She puts her reading glasses down on the table.

'Yes, of course,' he replies. 'That's the whole idea.'

She seems to be forcing herself to meet his eye.

'But that lovelessness, that anger with the person who's . . .'

'Well,' he interrupts. 'It's just that the priest is a bit shut off, you see.'

'But you're not shut off,' she says, leaning forward so the cushion falls down behind her back.

'If I'd become a priest, though . . .'

'Sorry. It's just that it doesn't feel very nice,' sighs Käbi. 'His wife is dead and Ingrid Thulin is his lover.'

'What the hell . . .?' he says, going over and snatching the script from her hands.

He doesn't look at her as she stands up and takes a

few steps. Doesn't meet her gaze when it seeks his.

Just runs a hand through his dirty hair.

And hangs his head a little, scratches the back of his neck, returns to put the script on the table by the armchair where she was just sitting.

He knows he has got to talk to her, goes over and touches her thick hair, feels his way under it, gently, to her damp neck.

'Haven't you got to rush off to the read-through?'

'Yes,' he replies, and feels her slipping out from under his hand. A movement that both accentuates and terminates his caress.

She walks past her Bechstein grand and sits down silently at her Steinway; after a moment she plays the first porcelain tinkle of Beethoven's sonata number 30.

But lingeringly, with the right pedal down.

Letting the notes extend, undampered. Letting them run into each other and blend, like watercolours.

Ingmar changes down, swings round the old silent film studios with a crunch of wheels and stops, facing the brick wall of the offices.

The sky is sealed, like a sheet of opal glass just above the rooftops.

He leaves the car unlocked, runs indoors and up the stairs to the third floor.

Comes to a halt outside the first door, but not really from a need to get his breath back.

Fingerprints cluster restlessly round the door handle. A coarse carpet exudes an intense smell of sun-warmed rubber.

He imagines himself going in and meeting his ensemble in the foyer of the Small Studio, being depressed by their jokes and their attempts to sound appreciative when he tells them to be honest. But at the same time he'll be aware of their concern that he will disturb their work on their roles by anticipating the process, a concern combined with awareness of the risk that he will interpret their need to cocoon themselves as unwillingness.

And yet they must meet, must somehow begin their coming together.

He wonders which of the actors will take responsibility for making the read-through a properly functioning, maybe even pleasant, prelude. Ingrid and Gunnar, presumably. Max, but not Gunnel.

After almost two hours he brings the reading to a close; it is time for Allan to go to rehearsals at the Royal Dramatic Theatre.

'I'm not sure,' says Ingmar, wiping his sweaty palms on his trousers, 'but several of you don't really seem to understand the ending.'

'Understand may not be the right word.'

'You want to know how to interpret it. How I see it.'

'Yes.'

'Then I'd better tell you about when my father and I drove round to visit a whole lot of churches in Uppland last spring. One Sunday we found ourselves in a little medieval church just north of Sigtuna. There were a few people sitting inside. The church-warden and the verger were whispering in the porch. A quarter of an hour after the bell stopped ringing, the priest arrived, out of breath. He'd overslept. Said he was ill, had a temperature. But when he announced that the service would be curtailed, Father stood up in his pew . . .

Ingmar smiles at the memory and is suddenly conscious of his lie.

He lowers his eyes and continues.

'So the long-haired priest came out of the vestry, followed by Father in white vestments: Holy, holy, holy is the Lord of Hosts, and so on. I mean, I'd already written the whole script; the only thing missing was the ending. And then I got this from my father. Like a gift. An old priest's rule: come what may, you must hold your service. So I gave the priest in the film a choice. There are only two people in the congregation, perfectly legitimate grounds for cancelling the service. But he decides to go ahead regardless, for his own sake, for Märta's, for . . .'

Afterwards, Ingmar would remember being met in the foyer of the Small Studio by a stench of cattle and urine. The October light fell through the tall windows, glittering on the aluminium frames, making the small dust particles gleam, languid as honey in their twirling.

When he got home, he told Käbi it had gone quite well.

But found it a real effort not to cry from sheer exhaustion as he lay with his head in her lap and told her how they had all been sitting round the table, ready.

'I thought that rather than going through the whole script, we'd concentrate on a few key scenes,' repeats Ingmar.

A pencil fell to the floor.

'Katinka can read the set and action descriptions,' he says softly, then stops.

Ingmar wakes in the middle of the night and sees an image of himself coming into the foyer, taking a big step over the heap of excrement just inside the door. There are a few crumpled paper plates on the plastic floor. A pile of paper napkins and a half-eaten apple.

A horse, resting its great head on the green baize cloth on the rickety table, follows him with a heavy eye.

One of the two ewes looks pregnant. There's a fly crawling in the sticky corner of her eye.

Ingmar apologizes for being a little late, then begins as usual by telling them he is probably the only person in the film world who holds joint read-throughs.

'In the theatre they're absolutely standard. But I've never seen the difference — after all, there's collective responsibility in films, too.'

A curly horn scrapes the corner of the table as the ram almost falls off his chair. One back leg kicks spasmodically until he regains his balance.

Ingmar pushes the cover off his sweaty body, listens to Käbi's calm breathing in the darkness beside him and no longer feels sure he has the energy to convince everyone that the film's got to be made, that it's important.

He closes his eyes and sees in his mind's eye the pregnant ewe tearing and kicking the pages of the script with her hooves.

'Do you all agree that the priest has already been demolished before the film opens? Well, what I — mean by demolished is that he does his job perfectly on the surface, and yet . . . This is where I can visualize myself as a priest. I'd write my sermons, just as my father does, I'd talk about having faith, but . . .'

She munches on a pencil, chews with saliva dripping from her mouth and then rests her chin on the soft tablecloth and closes her eyes.

'Not exactly the Four Horsemen of the Apocalypse then,' Ingmar had said with a smile, addressing himself to the other ewe.

There were wet autumn leaves caught in her dirty

grey fleece. Muddy knots dangling around her haunches and tail.

Ingmar knows that he leant forward, looked into the ewe's blank eyes and tried to describe how loveless the teacher's liaison with the priest was.

How painful every encounter proved to be.

Almost comically so.

Then suddenly he realized she wasn't understanding a word he said, stopped and began all over again.

'So you see, from a distance, in her solitude, when the teacher writes her letters, the relationship is full of love,' he explained.

There was a glimpse of teeth under the cleft lip.

'But when the priest is exposed in the letters to this naïve love, which she otherwise has the sense to keep hidden, it turns his stomach. Do you see? He could literally throw up over her.'

When he has been lying awake for a while, staring up at the black, sagging ceiling, he hears Käbi grope for the glass of water on her bedside table and drink.

'Käbi, can I just say one thing?' he asks quietly.

'What is it?' she mumbles.

'Are you asleep?'

'Of course I am, but . . .'

'I won't disturb you.'

A deep breath, lips moistened by a tongue.

'Is it important?'

'No.'

She sits up.

'What's on your mind?' she asks.

'I don't know, well lots of things, all . . .'

He stops and reaches for her hand, straight out into the darkness.

'Shall we get up for a while?' she asks.

'You do know,' he says, 'that I'm not taking Father into account? I never have done.'

'What do you mean by taking into account?'

'It's never been, how shall I put it, I've never had him specifically in mind when I've been making my films, doing my plays.'

'You should just forget him.'

'I know. It's not something I think about.'

'What is it then?'

'Just that, when I woke up,' he says hesitantly, 'I thought I was lying in bed beside Ellen, it took a second for me to realize where I was, you know, and my heart was pounding like . . .'

'What's making you think about Ellen?'

Ingmar shuts his eyes for a moment.

'When the twins were born, I more or less stopped going home; I couldn't cope with it. Claimed I needed my sleep to be able to write. Peace and quiet and so on. Now, all I can think about is what hard work it must have been for her, on her own with four children. And what was she supposed to think? I mean, I was hardly ever there.'

'Because you'd met Gun Grut?'

'I remember deciding all of a sudden to tell her the truth.. We hadn't seen each other for two weeks when I went round. She was already in bed, but she was so incredibly pleased that she wanted to open a bottle of wine, cook me a meal, only . . .'

He sighs.

'Her face when she suddenly sensed my impatience and realized I'd come for a reason. Käbi, I don't know, I think what happened that night – it feels as if I need to get back to it. To that moment, that difficult moment when the lying ends.'

Ingmar still cannot see Käbi's face in the bed.

'Are you awake?'

'Yes I am,' she says under her breath.

6

In the hall, Ingmar hands his mother his coat, blinks in the darkness and says he has come straight from a press reception.

'What's happened?' she asks.

'No, nothing, it's just that we start filming tomorrow.'

'Filming?'

He rubs his hand under his nose.

'Can't we put the overhead light on?'

'It is on, you just have to feel your way.'

He is about to go in, but finds she is blocking his path, holding his heavy coat.

'Have you thought about Father's seventy-fifth birthday?' she asks softly.

'I'm afraid I can't make it, nor can Käbi.'

'It'll just be the two of us, then,' she says, switching on a wall light; its gleam blossoms like a blue lily against black glass.

They start picking their way down the hall, cautiously so as not to trip. The darkness vibrates softly before their eyes, with aggressive spasms, and then reverts to being merely flat.

'I could treat you to a week at Siljansborg.'

'That's fine by me,' she replies, locating the

doorpost with her hand. 'But Father's an old sour-puss, as you used to say when you were little.'

'I can't see a bloody thing,' he mutters. 'This is ridiculous.'

'You get used to it.'

A porous disc of sun is reflected in the dust on the window, but its glimmer does not penetrate to the lounge. And the faint light from the chandelier is soaked up by the vast blackness of the oil painting.

'Of course, it was much nicer having Hedvig Eleonora church right outside.'

'It's a totally crappy flat,' she says with a broad smile.

The study door creaks and Erik emerges, coughing.

'Putte's here,' says his wife.

'Oh,' he says, and goes over to the window.

'We're sitting at the table.'

Ingmar's father appears as a vague outline against something beaded and grey. Erik holds his old pocket watch to his ear.

'No,' he sighs, looks at it and twiddles the knob at the top.

Ingmar's mother says these rooms remind her of when they moved from the house at the ironworks in Forsbacka to an apartment at 27 Skeppargatan.

Her mouth twitches.

'I was heavily pregnant, and I sat down on one of these chairs and cried, I recall. Which may have been a bit of an over-reaction. If you compare it to this. Anyway, as soon as you were born we fled up to Duvnäs, just so we could breath. I remember that time. All the light, quite amazing . . . you were almost a month old before we suddenly realized we ought to baptize you.'

Ingmar stops biting his thumbnail.

'It was Father who baptised . . .'

Erik coughs.

'I remember being so moved,' he says. 'Getting the Lord's Prayer wrong when I baptised Dag, but . . .'

He stops, comes slowly towards them, sits down in the armchair and puts the pocket watch on the table. His hand rests in the thin gleam round the china lamp base.

'It's stopped,' he says. 'But the balance-wheel is working.'

'Is there something wrong with your watch?'

'Listen for yourself.'

Ingmar's father gropes for the pocket watch on the table, his hands moving cautiously, feeling in the dark.

'Hopeless,' he mumbles.

'When I was working on the script, Father,' says Ingmar, 'I often thought of some lines from a poem you wrote. Help me ever dutiful, and white as snow in my heart, to turn to each allotted task, as if I owned and saw Thee.'

'I'm going for my evening walk,' Erik tells his wife, lowering his voice.

Ingmar gets up and murmurs:

'Mmm, that might be nice.'

'No, you stay with your mother,' his father says, leaving the drawing room.

The leaves of the fern rustle briefly as the air moves. There is the sound of a running tap, then a soft thud of something falling over.

Ingmar feels on the table for the watch, fingers the runner covering the deep scratch in the surface. The ceiling creaks and the light wavers even more. Karin is talking in her loneliness about Nitti, the fact that she has no idea how she is getting on over in England and has not heard from her for a long time.

A coat hanger hits the floor and skids under the hall table with a clatter.

'Just got to ask Father something,' says Ingmar feebly.

He gets up, moves forward with one arm stretched out in front of him, reaches the wall, follows it to the left as far as the hall door, gets down on his knees, fumbles on the floor and finds the coat hanger.

'Can't I come with you?'

'I want to be left alone,' mumbles his father.

'Only I thought we could talk about the script.'

'I haven't read it,' Erik says bluntly. 'Because I take no interest in your films, to be honest. They are not art as far as I'm concerned. Do you understand? I do not share your view of human nature . . .'

In the light from the stairwell as the door slams shut between them, Ingmar can see that his father's cheeks are red.

Slow steps are heard, the gate of the lift. Ingmar

throws the hanger on the floor, squeezes his smarting eyes shut and runs with the other children across the grey-green ice of the river. He catches sight of the man who fell through, dark as a log, eyes open wide.

Ingmar's mother has taken off the lampshade and is shaking the standard lamp as he comes back in. She looks sad and waves him to the seat beside her, just as the light dims again.

'Time for the sofa?' he asks, before feeling his way round the table and sitting down.

'Father disapproves of virtually everything at the moment,' she says.

'But then he's always been impossible to talk to.'

'I know that's why you want him to read your script,' she answers quietly.

'It was just an idea, you see, portraying myself as a priest,' he says. 'As the priest I would have become if I'd let myself be guided by Father. I mean . . . I know it's tough for him to look at my script and then speak up and say maybe it was for the best, my choosing a different career.'

'But it isn't that easy for him to . . .'

'What do you mean, not easy?'

'I'm not defending Father.'

'No.'

'No actually, I'm not,' she says calmly. 'But it isn't easy for him, because the priesthood is just Father's way of trying to repay his debt to his mother for not passing his higher school-leaving examinations. Pardon me smiling, but . . . you know, she worked all those extra hours so he could go to school.'

'I know.'

'Let me tell you something . . . Sit down, dear. I want to . . . I've often thought of telling you this, but I was always afraid it would come out wrong.'

'What?' asks Ingmar curtly.

'A few days after the premiere of *Frenzy*, Father told me . . .

'You're under no obligation to help . . .'

'Can't you just listen to me?' she breaks in gently.

'All right.'

'You know when they were restoring Hedvig Eleonora they wanted to commission a new baptistry window? Everybody had their own ideas about the subject, but the decision was Father's, and he asked the artist to do a picture of Christ with His hand on a child's head, under a birch tree.'

Karin dabs at the corners of her eyes.

'Father had drawn it as best he could – a meadow and the two figures – and he asked the artist to make the child a boy. "Because I was thinking of Ingmar the whole time," he told me. Did you know that? He was even going to give them one of these pictures of you as a child, and had taken it to the church with him, but then he felt too shy, he said; his shyness caught up with him.'

* * *

Ingmar turns up the car heating as he drives to Djursholm; the stale air coming through the plastic grille is hot, but he is still freezing cold.

The roads are almost empty at this time of night.

Drizzly rain detaches itself from the darkness as it meets the windscreen. Tiny, luminous pins, swept away by the wipers.

He starts thinking about the baptistry window again, about the boy's lifeless face.

Suddenly the headlights of the car fill a bus shelter with their white gleam. For just a few seconds, the block of light hangs at the roadside, among tossing black branches. Yet Ingmar has time to register the woman on the bench, the rounded back of her hand and the timetable above her head.

He brakes carefully, changes down, slows, pulls in and stops.

The stretch of road through the patch of forest is virtually black.

He tries to make something out in the rear-view mirror, but the bus shelter has vanished into darkness. The treetops are silhouetted against the slightly paler sky. Distant lamplight from some house glimmers through the tree trunks.

He drums on the steering wheel. Rain falls through the light in front of the car. The tarmac glistens in a soft curve and disappears off behind trees and a dark, industrial building.

There's something about the woman in the bus

shelter, her plump body or downcast eyes perhaps, that reminds Ingmar of the wet-nurse from his fantasy about the flat. From the evening when he imagined there was a hole in the wall behind the linen cupboard, leading to an adjoining flat, soon to be demolished.

Now he's unsure whether there really was an opening in the wall. He remembers clearing up plaster and scraps of wallpaper from the floor the next morning, but thinks that might be part of the fantasy, too.

There's a slight crunching sound from behind the car.

He stops drumming on the steering wheel, tries to make something out in the rear-view mirror but it is all too dark, and he is wondering whether to reverse when the back door is wrenched open. He turns and sees the woman trying to get out of her wheelchair into the car. Instinctively he steps on the gas, lets out the clutch and swings out into the road, changes up and peers into the mirror, his heart thumping.

'What the hell was that?' he mutters.

Sweat pours from his armpits and down the sides of his body. With a shaking hand he turns off the fan, wipes his mouth.

He tries to think about the first day of filming, what happens in the vestry, the opening shots, but darkness keeps getting in the way.

A black, quivering surface behind milky-white window glass.

Just before Stocksund, he is forced to restrain an

impulse to cross the middle line and meet the bus from Norrtälje head-on.

* * *

Ingmar takes the script with him from the study, goes downstairs and sits at the dining table. Slow, repetitive octave practice can be heard through the wall from the music room.

He looks out at the old fruit trees in the darkness.

Initially he had thought the first take should include the barred window, the crucifix and the collection money all at once.

But now he tells himself it isn't really necessary. He mustn't get bogged down in the composition, the detail. The idea of the image within the image. Of peripheral symbolism.

The only thing that matters is staying true to the feeling of himself as a priest.

The piano notes have died away; he hears steps cross the parquet floor behind his back with a dry clacking sound. Käbi sits down on the sofa. The scratch of a nail drawn rapidly over rough fabric. And the restless motion of a fringed hem.

'I'm stopping now, too,' he mumbles, leafing through to find and check a couple of sentences in a piece of dialogue he is unsure about.

'Are you feeling stressed?'

'It's just that I want to be prepared,' he says.

'Because I need more than ever for the filming to run smoothly. I mean, I know lots of things always crop up, but I had to estimate low this time, and we haven't got quite as much money as we need.'

'Well, you'd better explain that to everybody.'

'Yes,' he sighs, closing the script. 'Or we'll just have to see how it turns out.'

As Ingmar gets up, he registers that the sofa is empty and his eye is simultaneously caught by a quick movement across the green grass outside.

Then he sees Käbi through the smoked glass tabletop. She's lying on the floor to rest her back.

'Have you seen that cat hanging round our garden?'

'No.'

Ingmar sits down.

'Seems to think she lives here,' he says under his breath, remembering when he mowed the grass the day before they left for Torö. The sharp smell of the apples as the steel blades cut the tiny unripe fruits that had fallen. And the cat, suddenly moving awkwardly and sideways.

'You know I lived in an open marriage with Gunnar,' Käbi says. 'I think he slept with every pretty violinist in the whole . . .'

'Yes, you told me.'

'But we didn't do anything to hide it,' she goes on. 'We didn't lie to each other, we told one another exactly . . .'

'But I could never stand it like that,' he stops her.

'A marriage where neither side tells lies?'

He stretches down one hand and feels the coolness of the tight space between the cushion and the upholstered arm.

'There's no way I could accept you sleeping with anybody else,' he answers. 'Call me old-fashioned and everything, but when you've been brought up in a vicarage . . .'

'That doesn't mean you automatically *become* a vicar,' she says, her voice raised. 'I've come to realize that for your parents, external appearance was the only thing that ma . . .'

'Stop!' he roars, bringing the underside of his clenched hand down on the table, so the thick sheet of glass gives a dull sigh and the bowl of apples shudders.

'I just think you overestimate lying,' says Käbi coolly.

'What am I supposed to say to that?'

'You'll vanish into your filming from tomorrow, and we'll scarcely see each other for the rest of the year.'

'You know that's a bit of an exaggeration.'

'But I want you to tell the truth when we do manage to be together; I don't want you to put it off until the filming's over,' she says.

Ingmar closes his eyes and feels inclined to remind her that he was the one who said he wanted children.

He is suddenly put in mind of the insidious interrogations that were routine in his childhood. When everything that could be considered a lie was to be extracted with a caress.

'Think I'll go to bed,' he mumbles.

She tries to catch his eye through the distorting lens of the glass table.

'No need to be angry,' she says softly.

'No, but I do wonder what you think you're doing.'

'Sorry, I only wanted to . . .'

'If we're being truthful now,' he goes on. 'Because I think in fact it's you who isn't being entirely honest.'

'But I am.'

'You say that, but if you don't . . .'

'Please stop,' she says, her voice suddenly tearful. 'I just get so scared sometimes that we'll lose each other.'

His eye is caught by the prisms of the chandelier, reflected next to the fruit bowl. A star formation, like radiating cracks in thick ice.

'But listen, Käbi. I do want to have a baby with you, you know . . . are you saying that's a lie?'

He leans over the table, reaches under it, strokes her head with his fingertips, her thick hair, and feels an anxiety in his stomach as he sees her relieved smile through the reflections in the glass.

7

A garden gnome from the south of Germany is standing in the bedroom, right in the middle of the carpet.

Ingmar wonders if Käbi thought he would laugh when he woke up.

Suddenly the gnome is up on the bed. Plodding across the thick quilt. Settling on Ingmar's lap as if to sleep, then shuffling back down to the floor again.

The fantasy begins to replay itself: Ingmar imagines the garden gnome has zinc paste on its lips and, instead of a cap on its head, a handkerchief knotted at the corners. The gnome pulls out a book that has been lying in the dust under the bed, turns to page eighty-seven and expects Ingmar to start reading:

The director steps into the light and the silence of Studio Five. In the middle of the vast floor stands the vestry, way below the intersecting steel girders of the roof trusses.

There is a strong smell of new paint, glue and freshly sawn wood.

He goes on, across the carpet, round the colourless back with its struts and beams, and is then able to see through the low, stone door into the church's inner-most room.

'I don't know,' he says, his voice scarcely audible. 'I'd been thinking we'd do it face to face, but in the car on the way here . . .'

He has to close his eyes for a moment, and immediately hears the murmuring. The cables running along the floor, the whispers.

Senses the larger space being filled out, then the smaller one; swaying, he feels the many movements envelop his body.

The cold water of the brook flowing around his legs.

'In the car on the way,' he whispers, then tails off.

Suddenly hears people talking around him, close to him. And knows he'll have to open his eyes soon.

'I've got to find out if there's a zoom lens for a self-blimping Arriflex,' someone says.

'No, we're starting with collodion on the nose.'

'Ask Skaar, there might be one for De Brie.'

Ingmar leans against the wall for support and sits down, sees their faces turn towards him and realizes his eyes are no longer shut.

'In the car on the way here,' he goes on, 'I was think-ing we could string it all together into a single scene.'

He points to the desk, the angle.

'The churchwarden here. And then Gunnar from there – the camera stays fluid, over to there and then back to here, right? Would that work?'

'I think so,' replies Sven.

'Over there and out a bit and then . . .'

Sven nods, squats down and scratches his sandy hair.

'Åland,' he says. 'That means we'll have the camera here.'

'To pan over to here.'

'Then we'll have to move the wall?' queries Åland.

'And all this other stuff,' Sven answers. 'Probably just as well.'

'Can you all hurry it up a bit please.'

The points of his uneven teeth glint momentarily before his face resumes its earnest expression.

Ingmar knows he ought to stay calm, and goes to sit in the director's chair.

He can't rush this.

Technical preparations and rehearsals before the first camera setting will take all morning, he knows.

Ingmar tries to sound cheerful as he approaches a couple of hands standing with Stig Flodin in the smoking area.

'So that's all we've got left?' he asks. 'A little beep?'

'Which is synchronized with a white square,' answers Stig.

'Have you heard this?'

Gunnar comes over.

'They've abolished the clapperboard,' continues Ingmar with a smile. 'Long live the . . . what was it called?'

'Light clapperboard.'

'Long live the light clapperboard!' he says, beaming. 'Don't you see? No more chalk dust flying. That'll make a nice change!'

Gunnar gives a hint of a smile.

'And that bloody bang . . .'

'It's just a beep now.'

'It's a revolution,' he jokes.

Sven comes over to Ingmar to say they're ready for a try-out.

Against a background of the crucifix from *The Seventh Seal*, the churchwarden empties the collection bag into his hand.

The priest puts his thermos flask on the desk just as the churchwarden starts counting the coins. Then puts his coffee cup on the blotter before he sits down.

He coughs, gets up again and goes to the window. Loiters there, his forearms resting on the high, sloping sill.

Ingmar is standing with shoulders tensed. His hair is straggly at the back of his neck and rather matted. The strain of concentration is making him bite his lower lip, giving his entire face a distorted, childish look.

When the churchwarden has finished counting, he asks the priest if he has found a housekeeper.

'You won't be able to manage in the long run.'

'Yes I will,' says the priest. 'I've managed for five

years, so I expect I can carry on for a while yet.'

The churchwarden writes the total in the cashbook.

'You could get Märta Lundberg to help you out. She'd like nothing better, you know. I could ask her for you.'

'No thank you,' the priest replies.

Then they both look up at the iron door as if they have heard a knock.

'Good,' says Ingmar, running his thumb and forefinger down the ridge of his nose. That was . . .'

Stig Flodin is standing in the darkness at the sound control console. He shakes his head and says Brian can't reach with the boom at the start of the dialogue.

'Why the devil not?' demands Ingmar. 'He's only got to stand there.'

'No, there's a shadow from the spotlight on . . .'

'The hell there is.'

Brian comes forward and tries it, but no matter how he angles the arm, it casts a shadow on the vestry wall.

'You're right,' concedes Ingmar. 'What shall we do? Couldn't you get closer from that direction?'

'Maybe a couple of centimetres.'

'We'll give it a try, but then I think we'll just have to press on.'

Ingmar stands on one side of Studio Five, watching all the people working on the scenery round the freestanding vestry. They shout to each other, shift a heavy section.

He is feeling the effects of having bolted his lunch. The boiled ham and fried egg are reluctant to settle down.

Cautiously, almost distractedly, Ingmar is talking to Kolbjörn Knudsen about moderating his tone of voice a little, a very little bit more. He presents it not as a problem, more as an idea, something worth trying. But Kolbjörn was anticipating criticism; he nods and his cheeks have a strangely taut look.

'Damn, I just knew it,' he mutters, crossing his arms over his chest.

'But it's sounding fine, even as it is,' explains Ingmar.

'I'm worried it'll just sound dull.'

'It won't, it won't.'

'In the theatre, you . . .'

'Exactly,' Ingmar interrupts. 'And quite right, too. There, you need variety the whole time. But this is film. And that means it's just fine the way you're doing it. It's enough, it may even be a bit too much; that's a possibility, which is why I want you to try taking it down just a touch more.'

He can see Gunnar is sceptical, and turns to him as well.

'I mean, this is bloody important – if we just get the tone right the first day, we can usually stick to it for the whole film.'

'What tone, though?' mumbles Gunnar.

'The one you're using, it's perfect.'

'But a bit less, eh?'

'We'll have to try it and see. How about that? We'll take our time and try things as we go.'

Gunnar attempts a smile and Ingmar casts a glance at Sven, who nods in reply.

Katinka looks at her watch.

'All right,' Ingmar says. 'How are we feeling? Ready for the first take?'

He can't look Gunnar in the eye any more.

'Quiet please. Take.'

A blanket descends on the whole studio, closing in like winter.

Someone is breathing more rapidly than the rest of them, but then imperceptibly adapts.

'Camera,' says Ingmar, almost pensively.

'Camera rolling,' answers Stig Flodin from the sound control console.

A loud beep is heard.

The churchwarden is emptying the collection bag into his hand and the priest is putting his thermos flask on the desk when a man suddenly flies through the air.

He glides in silence, a short distance from the ground.

It all happens very quickly. But they have time to see him, even so. At a slant, as if through water. The pale face.

He tries to land on his feet, but the angle he comes in at is too awkward, his shoes scarcely graze the floor, his legs slide away and his shoulder and hip take the impact.

People run over to him. He sits up.

'That was a hell of a kiss!' he mutters, his eyes empty.

'What happened, Kalle? Electric shock?'

'Think it was the camera light,' he says, trying to get up. 'It can't be soldered.'

Kolbjörn stands in the midst of the uproar, saying his lines to himself; he curses his own incompetence and starts all over again.

The electricians lift the steel-framed light mounting off the camera.

Ingmar walks off and sits on the floor, away from the others. Is aware of the after-effects of the increased cardiac activity making his hands shake.

He leans back against the wall and pale grey shadow fills the furrow running from the side of his nose past the corner of his mouth, into the old scar that over time has formed a dimple in his skin.

In the middle of the vast floor, figures are moving around the vestry, black cables being dragged unhurriedly. People stand and chat, light another cigarette.

For some reason, Ingmar starts to think about Strindberg writing *Swanwhite* specially for Harriet

Bosse, but then making sure it was Fanny Falkner who got the part.

Sven Nykvist signals that they are ready for another try. Ingmar looks at his watch and positions himself behind the camera in the vestry. He sees everyone resume their places, feels calm spreading, and when the light clapperboard beeps, the soft waves in the light begin:

'You look poorly,' says the churchwarden, and Ingmar can hear at once that he's got it wrong. Kolbjörn has lost the whole, absent tone they worked towards in rehearsals. He is keeping his chin pressed into his neck as they agreed, but his acting is theatrical.

Ingmar can see the panic in his eyes. The feeling of not being as good as the others.

The words are running through Gunnar: 'If I could just go and lie down . . .'

Kolbjörn holds the churchwarden's spectacles up to the light and polishes them.

'You could get Märta Lundberg to help you out,' he says. 'She'd like nothing better, you know. I could ask her for you.'

'No thank you,' the priest replies abruptly.

Both men suddenly look towards the iron door.

'Thank you,' says Ingmar, and scratches the back of his head.

Knowing that in a few seconds he's got to come up

with an acceptable lie to justify another take, without criticizing Kolbjörn.

Stig Flodin gives a thumbs-up from the sound desk.

Ingmar can see the actors are waiting for his reaction.

Kolbjörn tries to smile to himself.

'Well done, Gunnar,' says Ingmar. 'But I thought your "No thank you" was a bit too sharp, if you know what I mean.'

'No.'

His brow is shiny with perspiration.

Gunnar remains sitting at his desk in the vestry, waiting for an explanation. With a double furrow between his eyebrows and curiously thin lips.

'We'll take it once more,' says Ingmar. 'It may not be necessary, but we've plenty of time. Shall we? Gunnar?'

Gunnar gets to his feet, clears the flask and cup off the desk.

Silence.

'Camera,' shouts Ingmar.

'Camera rolling,' confirms Stig Flodin.

The light clapperboard beeps, the golden tassel of the collecting bag swings. Ingmar bites his thumbnail and is suddenly at Mäster Olofsgården after the premiere of *Swanwhite*.

The Germans had taken Paris, his mother was standing a little way from him in the foyer, coffee cup in hand, as the snow whirled outside the two windows.

'You look poorly,' said one of the actresses.

Ingmar ran his hand across his mouth, not meeting her gaze.

'If I could just go and lie down . . .'

A gentle shift runs through the group.

'And here we have the child prodigy,' a man says softly, bringing Harriet Bosse forward. A short woman, a little older than his own mother. But pretty, he had thought. With rounded cheeks, head held high.

And she had looked at him, taking her time, then asked with a smile:

'Did your mother and father come to see the play?'

'I've only seen Mother,' he replied, gesturing in his mother's direction.

'What did she think?'

'I don't know.'

'I could ask her.'

'No thank you,' replies the priest.

The actors look up at the door with its iron mountings.

'Thank you,' says Ingmar. 'Good. Really. Didn't you feel it all coming together? It just happened. Now we deserve a bit of cake, I think.'

He goes off with Sven, remembers he needs to speak to Katinka, comes back and happens to hear Gunnar through the thin wall of the church.

'But it's nothing to do with a special tone; he isn't trying to get it stylized or precise, all he wants is some goddamned mumble.'

Ingmar's cheeks burn, but he stops himself getting angry, rushing in.

I ought to throw him out, he thinks, and moves away. A tumbling anxiety churns in his stomach, swelling his intestines.

He stands still, waiting, not understanding what has happened. The grey gleam is suspended from the light fitting like worn linen cloth.

Like a distant cloudburst.

Dusty plastic sheeting from ceiling to floor.

The huge studio is silent, abandoned. A crumpled cigarette packet in a coffee cup.

He realizes it must be three in the morning, but continues even so.

In the middle of the empty floor area lie a man's black shoe and a magazine with pornographic pictures. As he bends down, something passes behind him. He turns round and is just in time to see naked flesh moving, disappearing behind the vestry. Out of the corner of his eye, the glimpse of a bottom, a solid thigh. Perhaps a couple of vertebrae along a back.

Then comes the sound of someone moving the simple desk in the vestry; its legs scraping the floor. He goes up to the door and listens. The desk shifts a little further, then something starts to creak.

Slowly but heavily.

Followed by sudden sighs, some grunts. Soil falling on a wooden surface.

The desk shuffles on, bangs against the door. Is raised slightly and dropped back onto the floor; scrapes against the door and is wedged there.

Ingmar lies down on the floor and tries to peer under the iron door. In the warm draught at floor level he is aware of an acrid, pungent smell.

It feels almost as if he has dozed off on the studio floor when he hears Stig Flodin laughing with Brian Wikström at the sound console. Ingmar gets to his feet and squints into the glare from the overhead lights, runs his hand over his hair.

'How did it look?' asks K.A. 'Do you want to raise the door?'

'No,' answers Ingmar.

His back is sweaty and he feels chilled.

K.A. is still there, drinking coffee from a mug with a dark-brown glaze.

The actors are standing with Sven and Åland as Ingmar comes over to the smoking area.

'Aren't we just? A fine collection of cheerful types,' says Gunnel, and sits down on the chair with her name on the back.

'And I'm definitely the funniest of the lot,' jokes Max.

'Until the suicide,' replies Gunnel, 'Then it's me with my big stomach.'

'At least neither of you has a cold,' ventures Gunnar.

Sven walks off towards the vestry.

'But seriously, it's not really that bad, is it?' says Ingmar. 'My father's read the script three times and he doesn't find it at all gloomy. I mean, it's not meant to be a comedy, after all.'

'But it's so goddamned grey and dreary,' says Allan with a smile.

'Who actually wants to see this film?' asks Gunnar. 'Apart from your father? What audience are we aiming at?'

Ingmar laughs and says he was in a queue of traffic the other day, looked into the other cars and thought: You won't go to see my film, you won't go to see my film, you won't go, and so on.

'Then maybe we ought to think again,' mumbles Allan.

Gunnar looks away, Max tries to appear unconcerned, and Gunnel says they mustn't underestimate the public.

Ingmar leaves his place alongside Sven behind the camera and goes over to the actors sitting at the priest's table.

'That was fine,' he says. 'But we'll do it again, with a bit more air.'

'What do you mean, air?' asks Gunnar.

'I mean we mustn't be too heavy at the start. Like when the *Andrea Doria* sank. What I mean is: the real horror comes later. And none of you knows that just at the moment. For now, let's hover between embarrassment and lack of contact. The thing is, none of you wants to be sitting here. Especially not you, Max. You think the whole situation's absurd, bothering the priest with . . .'

'Yes, that's how I see it.'

'This is quite an exciting scene, isn't it?' asks Ingmar. 'The priest talking to himself, so to speak?'

'It's my favourite scene,' says Gunnel.

'How very kind of you to say so,' jokes Ingmar.

'But I agree with her,' says Gunnar. 'I like the way I'm suddenly so afflicted by my own inability to convey any kind of will to live.'

'Exactly, that's exactly what happens. It's between the two of you. And you're in the middle, Gunnel. Without any way of realizing the seriousness of what's happening between the two men at this point.'

'In fact, I could show a touch of relief,' she says. 'At finally having taken the step, as it were.'

'Yes, good idea.'

'Because I'm feeling as if I've transferred some of the burden to the pastor.'

'Precisely,' says Ingmar, giving her a long look. 'Shall we try going through it one last time? What do you think? It's feeling pretty good, this, don't you think?'

Gunnar nods.

'And it's important for the whole thing to be in a completely ordinary tone,' Ingmar goes on. 'A sense of everyday Swedish reality. Nothing theatrical at all.'

Studio Five is filled with darkness. The only light falls through the vestry window, down onto the priest's desk.

While they were running through it, Stig Flodin had signalled that he was happy with the sound.

K.A. adjusts one of the chairs and then leaves the room.

Sven nods to Ingmar. Brian takes up his position.

Quiet please.

Ingmar realized when he got home from school that his mother was still in bed. The air remained untouched. A night-time mood persisted although the rooms were suffused with light.

He went to the kitchen to see if she'd had any breakfast. Thought perhaps he could go in and ask her if she wanted any coffee.

He waited outside her door, listening. Knocked discreetly, waited a little while and knocked again.

Then he sat down with his back against the wall. Saw little balls of fluff travelling along the floorboards. Scampering along the corridor and disappearing into a slice of sunlight from the window in Nitti's room.

He scratched a mosquito bite, felt the size of the bump with his thumb and forefinger.

The ornamental clock struck, to be followed by the subterranean echo from the clock on the Engelbrekt church.

A movement could be heard from his mother's room. She must have picked up the glass of water from her bedside table, drunk some and put it back.

Ingmar got up, knocked carefully and went into the saturated air.

'What are you doing here, Putte?'

I only wanted to help her, thinks Ingmar. She always used to be glad when I asked her if she and I could talk about all the beautiful things, all the things she and I like: opera, theatre, art.

'I feel so impotent. I don't know what to say. I understand your anguish. And yet we have to live.'

'Why do we have to live?' retorts Jonas with a directness that surprises even himself.

The priest lowers his eyes.

After a moment there is a hint of cheerfulness, perhaps even victory, in Jonas's face.

'Pastor, you're sick and shouldn't be sitting here talking to me. We're not getting anywhere, anyway.'

The air in Studio Five is warm and heavy. Circulates slowly away from the static heat of the spotlights. Turns to the tall walls, bringing with it the yeasty, honey scent of the carpet to the silent people round the set.

'Thank you,' says Ingmar, wiping the perspiration from his top lip. 'Perfect. That was . . . That was bloody good.'

'Aren't we going to take it again?' asks Gunnar.

'No need,' Ingmar replies.

The actors look relieved, almost surprised. They glance at each other.

A few people clap and Åland opens the great studio doors; cool air floods in, together with a gentler, different light.

Ingmar and Gunnar go out onto the loading platform, stand beside each other in the flat sunshine and look out over the light-drenched foliage of the autumnal trees. Inhale deeply, feel the fresh air on their faces.

Ingmar looks sideways at Gunnar, who is standing there in his cassock, loosening his yellow collar a little.

A deep score gouged by some piece of scenery in transit runs the length of the sloping platform.

Ingmar follows Gunnar's gaze to a flock of yellow buntings eddying up like sediment from the ring of yellow leaves under the maple.

*   *   *

Ingmar holds the doorpost to steady himself, pauses for

a few seconds and surveys the colourless palisade of the church, the sturdy struts against the walls of scenery.

The kind you have for keeping too large a herd of cattle in check, he thinks, stepping over cables and bunches of wires taped together and limping past a box that once contained film cassettes. He moves slowly through the cleared studio, but it's so painful just below the knee that he has to stop and sit down on one of the chairs in the smoking area.

He pulls up his trouser leg and realizes he had forgotten about his prosthesis.

Can do nothing but stare at the grey plastic leg, the casing, the shiny turn of the ankle.

It's inconceivable, and yet his hands move with great assurance as they undo the straps, unhook the leg and massage the sweaty stump.

Max comes in with an open bottle of champagne; he winks, takes off his false lower arm and fills the cavity with wine. Ingmar laughs and holds out his leg, Max fills it and they toast each other.

Ingmar is sitting in the darkness of the big screening room between Sven and Stig Flodin. He is still feeling a bit tipsy and smiles to himself. The rushes from the first takes are ready.

In the rectangle of light with its rounded corners, the great crucifix on the vestry wall is in shot; the velvet bag is emptied out into a hand and the thermos flask placed on the desk.

The priest sits down, coughs and goes over to the window.

'What the hell's up with the sound?' whispers Ingmar.

He gets up and looks towards the projection room.

'Wait a second,' suggests Stig.

He sits down and sees the churchwarden polishing his spectacles, holds his breath as he talks to the priest about solitude.

'Makes the vestry sound like a bloody tin can,' Ingmar says as the reels are being changed.

'Let's hear the next one.'

'Are you ready?'

'Hurry up.'

The collecting bag again, the thermos flask and the priest going over to the window. The forefinger moving coins across the table, then the spectacles against the November light.

'It sounds bloody awful, doesn't it?' says Ingmar. 'We'll have to shoot the whole lot again.'

Stig rubs his face with his hands and whispers, 'Damn, damn, damn.'

There's a low murmur of voices, discussions of the light clapperboard.

Ingmar feels his pulse starting to race.

'What? You think that might be the problem?'

'Don't know,' replies Stig.

'Well we can't do anything else until we know,' says Ingmar, raising his voice. 'I'm not blaming anybody, but this is going to cost a hell of a lot of money; it'll cost in studio time, it'll cost in wages.

'I'll go and ring AGA straight away.'

'Good idea Stig,' says Ingmar and bites his thumbnail. 'You do that.'

He watches Stig go. The dark, tousled hair. Thinks it was a good job he didn't lose his temper.

'It'll get sorted out,' mutters Ingmar, taking a seat beside Sven. 'And the photography, the lighting . . . that was all perfect.'

'Did you think so?' Sven asks with a big smile. 'I think it's good, too.'

'Can you do it all over again when we re-shoot the whole fucking thing?'

'Yes, I think so.'

Ingmar scratches his neck and tries to compose himself. He stands at the editing table feeling as if he'd like to knock it over. Trample things underfoot. Scream at someone and run out of the studio.

He grabs the script to tear it up and catches sight of the box of Droste chocolates. The film pulled taut over the unopened box; the wet sheen of cellophane across the dark lid.

He realizes Katinka must have got in her car, driven somewhere, bought the chocolate and put it on his desk.

'And what do you say?' he mumbles, and starts leafing through the script.

He sinks onto his chair and looks at the scenes that

will have to be done again because of the faulty sound. Memorizes the pitch levels that will need recreating, searches for dips it might be possible to fill.

A man in a light grey suit is standing at the sound board with Stig and Brian.

A fringe of gingery beard framing his chin and a pair of glasses in his hand.

Ingmar watches them, but waits until they have said their goodbyes and the man has left Studio Five before he goes over and picks up a five öre coin from the floor.

'What did he say?'

Stig is so relieved that there are tears in his eyes as he reports that they have already found and rectified the problem: the light clapperboard was connected wrongly.

'He told you that?'

'Yes, and he tested . . .'

'And you're sure it was the light clapperboard that was the culprit?'

'AGA didn't just send any old engineer,' Stig replies. 'I mean, if the inventor himself tells you the light clapperboard messed up the sound . . .'

They look at each other, and break into smiles.

'So we can get on now?' asks Ingmar.

'Yes, fire away.'

Still alone at his table on the canteen veranda, Ingmar eats his boiled ham with egg and potato, hunched over his plate.

An open window tugs listlessly at its catch. Black iron shows through where the white paint has flaked off. The curtain moves gently in the draught.

He looks down the slope and away through the trees. In the cold air, the light is like glass. Scratched across red Virginia creeper and brickwork.

He puts down his fork and suddenly smells cigarette smoke. Someone has stopped under the veranda window in mid-conversation; feet crunch in the gravel and there is an audible belch.

'There are always technical problems with Ingmar's shoots, never any other time.'

'Yeah, I've noticed,' says a younger man.

'It's probably because he always has to interfere in everything, you know, coming over with his bloody: Hello lads, this is looking great, but . . .'

'Yes, but you'll be . . . Stop it!' laughs a third. 'After this shoot even you lot will be bragging . . .'

They boo loudly and a tired voice answers something Ingmar can't catch. The window hook strains at its eye. A cigarette end is flipped away and lands in the gravel.

In the canteen, cutlery slides off a plate, down among the rest, to a jagged, multi-bladed response.

The sweet aroma of coffee heralds the arrival of Birger Juberg. He puts his cup down on the table and pulls out a chair.

'I've just heard you've got to start all over again,' he says amiably.

'No, but that bloody light clapperboard did ruin the sound,' Ingmar replies.

'Then surely you'll have to re-shoot the lot?'

'Yes, but . . .'

'Well, won't you?'

'But lighting, rehearsals . . .'

'I spoke to Allan yesterday – and he thought you were going to find it hard to stay within budget, even as it was, never mind running off to play about with weird clapperboards.'

'It's fixed now.'

'Whoopee,' says Birger, fumbling for his shirt pocket and taking out a packet of cigarettes. 'But if you think you won't be able to manage without extra funds, I'd rather you said so now.'

They sit looking at each other, aware that their relative positions have shifted since Birger took over from Dymling.

'You want me to beg,' says Ingmar gravely.

Birger leans back in his chair.

'No, I'm just saying . . .'

'And I'm happy to,' Ingmar goes on, tapping his plastic leg. 'More than happy. Shall I do that? Get down on my knees?'

He takes Birger's right hand in his.

'Stop messing about.'

'No, I'm going to kiss it.'

Birger tries to withdraw his hand and gives a surprised laugh when Ingmar won't let go.

'Yes, I'm going to kiss your hand and . . .'

'You can't . . .'

Ingmar kisses his hand and kneels down.

'Please, Birger,' he says, smiling. 'I beg you for a teensy weensy bit extra. Just to make sure . . .'

'No, it can't be done.'

Ingmar kisses his hand again.

'Please.'

He jerks free, but Ingmar grabs his leg instead.

'Stop it,' he whispers, looking towards the canteen.

'I'm going to kiss your feet,' laughs Ingmar. 'Every little piggy shall have a kiss.'

The chair overturns behind Birger. He stumbles and gropes for something to hold on to.

Ingmar locks the toilet door with trembling hands; the light of the fluorescent tube on the ceiling unfurls in four flickering gasps.

There's a smell of pig droppings. Paper towels lie scattered on the wet floor. The tap over the wash-basin runs silently.

Ingmar can feel his sweaty shirt against his back as he tears off a bit of toilet paper and wipes the yellow droplets from the seat.

He sits down and a new spasm of low, cramping pains makes him bend over his knees and tense his ankles and toes.

Someone rattles the door.

He leans against the cistern again, shuts his eyes,

feels embarrassed, fragile, hot in the face with anxiety. Wipes the sweat from his top lip and feels as if he could fall asleep at this moment.

Someone is running between the cubicles, hammering on all the doors. Then there are other footsteps, heavier. The fluorescent strip light on the ceiling goes out. Its aluminium fittings tick. Shouts penetrate the walls.

Someone is trying to unscrew the lock on the toilet door. Sharp metal against metal, a scraping sound very close by. A tool slips and engages again. The handle turns and the mechanism gives a click.

Then it all happens very fast.

He is dragged along the corridor, carried. Blinded by the gleam around the glass globes of the ceiling lights. Doors swing open and then shut. Ingmar fights against it, wants to see their faces. He turns his head, tries to twist round, but all he can see in any direction are backs.

He is left on a chair, blinking in the softer light. Sees the boar, hunch-backed, hooves scratching about among the coins on the desk.

The goat rolls the thermos flask along the floor.

The camera is running, pans gently, pulls back. The light falls on the goat's hairy cheek. Its eyes are lowered; its mind is searching for a way out.

Its nose is running continuously.

The boar's chin is tucked into its neck; the coarse

skin is creased. Its voice is as if shut inside that great chest, rattling. Its long canines glint yellow in its dry jaws.

To Ingmar they appear to be in disguise, wearing masks over masks.

The goat looks up at the iron door. The pig's eyes turn in the same direction.

Then they start again; the goat shakes itself and its collar falls to the floor. Ingmar says nothing. The pig presses its snout down on the collecting bag, drags it along while backing away.

'Quiet please. Take,' he whispers.

A thin sawblade goes straight through the half-metre thick wall of blocks of split granite. Glides downwards, meeting scarcely any resistance.

The sound changes as it hits a joist, sawdust pumps up in heavy cascades.

The section containing the deep window niche is folded back and carried away.

Nails screech and floorboards are torn up.

Suddenly, Sven can be seen through the opening; he points and moves aside.

Then silence again. Peter Wester whispers something and indicates his own shoulder and cheek.

Ingmar goes to Ingrid's position and asks Sven if it is all right.

'Yes.'

He moves.

'How does it look?'

'Fine,' comes Sven's quizzical reply.

Ingmar crouches and Sven nods.

'No problems, but . . . hang on a minute.'

He goes and looks through the camera.

'It looks good,' he mumbles.

'What do you say to the idea of doing the whole thing in a single take?' asks Ingmar, trying to hide his smile.

'Bloody great,' answers Sven, taken by surprise.

He moves one step to the side.

'Peter, sit in the chair.'

'Here?'

Sven squints. 'One take would be a real treat!'

'But if we lay rails,' says Ingmar. 'Then it might be . . .'

'It could turn out a bit cuckoo-clock mechanical,' Sven agrees. 'But we might be able . . .'

'What shall . . . Sorry, what did you want to say?'

'That we could try letting the camera dolly on Masonite boards.'

'Did you hear that, lads?'

They look at him.

'We're going to need a floor here that's totally bloody flat. From here – that's right isn't it, Sven? – right over to here.'

Ingmar is running along the corridor. Past the doors with the ribbed glass windows. Lenn is waiting by a dazzling lamp outside his room.

'Don't forget your meeting with Harald Molander,' says Lenn, opening the door.

Ingmar breathes rapidly through his nose and looks at the clock.

'Yes, what's up with him? Does he want the Big Studio back, or what?'

'No idea,' replies Lenn, going into the office.

Ingmar follows, sits down, picks up the telephone and answers.

'We've got to talk and sort this out once and for all,' his mother says. 'I ring you, but nobody answers. I'm trying to organize everything, but I get no response. Am I the only one who thinks it would be a shame if Father's big day were completely ruined?'

'But I'm in the middle of shooting a film and Käbi's got . . .'

'How can you be so harsh, Ingmar? I simply don't understand. It can't be that hard to take one day off.'

'I can't make it on the 22nd.'

'Why not?'

Lenn has started typing, outside the glass door.

'I've got to go,' says Ingmar.

His mother is breathing slowly at the other end of the receiver.

'I simply don't know what to do,' she says, scarcely audible.

'Invite some friends round.'

'To make up for the lack of family, you mean?'

'There's no need for us to start arguing about this.'

He tries to open a letter with one hand. It's difficult, virtually impossible. Suddenly he can see the tensed creature in all its manual impotence.

'Yesterday evening I was telling your father about your film,' she says.

'Were you? Did he say anything?'

'Maybe ought to see that, he said.'

'What? Is that what he said?'

'I wasn't even sure he was listening,' she replies. 'Think I was saying the priest's work as a priest somehow gets in the way of his life.'

'And then Father said he wanted to see my film?'

'I don't know, perhaps he thought it reminded him of his time in Forsbacka.'

'Can't you tell me exactly what he said?'

The fizzy lemonade went up his nose and brought tears to his eyes. He looked at his father, saw it would be all right to laugh, and did laugh, thinks Ingmar, walking on into the vestry.

The carpenters still haven't laid the Masonite boards; they are sitting smoking, leafing through the big, over-white sheets of plans.

He goes over to them, wipes his hand across his mouth.

'How's it going?'

'Fine,' answers one.

Another gives an embarrassed grin.

Ingmar lowers his voice, without finding his way into any sort of anger. Feels too pleased about his father's interest.

'You've got ten minutes to get this floor down if you want to be kept on,' he says, hiding his sudden smile with his hand. 'I don't give a toss what the union says, and if I find even the tiniest unevenness in the joins or any other sloppy work, you'll be out like a flash, the whole lot of you.'

Ingrid kisses Gunnar on the mouth and on the cheek, in a kind of desperation, abandonment, before turning to Ingmar with a good-humoured look and asking if it's okay that she has kept her gloves on.

'Yes, that's good,' laughs Ingmar. 'Let's try it.'

'Shall I stay?' she asks.

'No thank you. There's no need.'

'Oh Tomas, there's so much you've got to learn.'

'If you say so, teacher,' comes the ironic reply.

'You've got to be incredibly feeble here,' Ingmar points out. 'Flat intonation. He's so damn tired of never being left alone. Whenever he says he's going anywhere, she asks if she can come too, and when he says she can't, she starts blubbing or whingeing like a bloody child.'

'By the way, have you read my letter?' Ingrid asks.

'Your letter?' Gunnar answers. 'No, I haven't had time . . .'

'No need for anything large-scale there,' says

Ingmar. 'We're so close up with the camera. Just a slight frown, that's enough.'

Gunnar doesn't reply; his face is averted, his lips turn even paler.

Ingmar squats down in front of the actors.

'Shall we give it a try? Being really dull?'

After Uncle Johan had devoted hours to reconstructing the picture magazine and lens of the cinematograph, he asked Ingmar a favour in return: to keep his pipe hidden in an absolutely safe place, where it would not be discovered and confiscated by Ma.

But the very next morning, there stood Dag with the pipe held high above his head, demanding with fear in his eyes that Ingmar poke a finger up the poodle's backside. He had tried, Teddy had whimpered anxiously, and then Dag had slowly broken the pipe in two.

Ingmar had screamed, attempted to hit his big brother and not even noticed he had wet himself until Dag started to laugh.

The rapid heartbeats resulting from the sudden warmth down his legs. Then the weight in his trousers and the warmth unexpectedly turning cold.

'Thanks for that,' says Ingmar with delight in his voice, and turns to the assistant cameraman. How many metres did we get there? A hundred and fifty?'

He checks: a hundred and fifty-seven.

A bird that has got into the studio slices up

through the air, falls heavily, sails and turns upward once more.

The dazzling rectangle with rounded corners pulsates on the screen. A trembling, luminous square. Then the light suddenly calls forth darkness, blackness: the priest's back, the shadow across the stone floor.

'What the hell is that?' roars Ingmar, and the words pass behind Sven and hit Brian, who knocks over a loudspeaker stand.

Ingmar scratches the back of his neck and looks at Brian – whose cheeks are red as he picks up the stand – before turning to Sven.

'There's some muck in the film trap, he says. When did it start? Did you see? After scene eighty, or when?'

'Bet it got in when we loaded the film,' sighs Sven.

'Bugger,' says Stig.

'It's nobody's fault, but this is bloody crazy,' mutters Ingmar. 'We'll have to shoot the whole damn thing again . . .'

Ingmar stands with his back to the film screen, moves along the wall towards the metal door.

Sven and Peter Wester are talking to each other, while Stig stares at the floor.

Lenn comes into the auditorium, waves to Ingmar and hurries over.

'You know Molander's sitting waiting in your room?'

Ingmar opens the screening room door.

'The meeting was supposed to start at . . .'

He goes out into the chilly air, hears the door shut behind him, walks round the Small Studio, past the outside staircase until he reaches his car. His hands are shaking so much he can't get the key in the lock.

'Fucking hell.'

He beats his clenched fist on the car roof. Strange, flat thuds echo against the brick wall. His heart carries on jolting in his chest.

*   *   *

Ingmar puts the dark blue socks on his bed and leaves the study in his bare feet. The imprints on the wax-yellow carpet fade as the fibres rise again.

He emerges into the reconciliation room and puts his martini glass on the table. Looks out through the French window to the balcony. The wet movement of leaves. In the light from downstairs. Apple-weighted branches swing in the gaps between the railings.

His eyes are stinging with fatigue.

Fingers through his untidy hair. His watch against the artery on his wrist.

The creased trousers, the grey sweater.

He realizes Käbi's eyes are following him; is aware of her on the far side of the Steinway.

She says she has left her drink in the bedroom

and then follows him when he goes to fetch it.

Stops at the door to the corner room.

The glass on the ledge under the tall mirror is almost empty. The twist of lemon high and dry, the olive gone.

She meets his gaze.

The headboard of the wide bed is upholstered in the same floral yellow chintz as the curtains. And the patterns are reflected, interlaced, in the little brass doors of the tiled stove.

Smiling, she comes over to him.

'Oh, had I already finished it?'

'Virtually.'

She takes his hand and puts it to her cheek.

He looks at her.

'What is it?' she says under her breath.

He puts down the glass.

'Nothing. It's just that I thought you had your period.'

'It finished yesterday,' she says quietly, but not in a whisper. She sits down in the pale blue Carl Malmsten armchair.

He stays where he is, twisting his wedding ring.

'I'm thirty-nine,' she says. 'Nothing's particularly regular any more, but I don't feel old.'

The collar of the jumper rubs the neck, digs into the red fur as the fox turns his head towards Käbi.

Tentatively she holds out the dish of salted

almonds and asks if Mickel wants to try them.

But instead the fox's eye is drawn to her hand and follows her arm up to the back of her neck.

She points to the oranges, but the eye doesn't move. The black slit lies still in its copper cloud. Fixed on the gentle beat of the gold chain against her carotid artery.

He makes an unexpected lunge. Käbi recoils and laughs. The fox collides with the glass table, its head disappears down into the knitted sweater, the arms grope about.

'Ow, that damn well hurts.'

Ingmar extracts the stuffed fox. He has cut himself on its claws. A pink line runs across his soft stomach and a necklace of little blood pearls suddenly appears.

'What have you done?'

He lets the sweater drop back and rubs his stomach.

'Tomorrow Sven and I are previewing *Through a Glass Darkly* at the Röda Kvarn – do you want to come?'

'Well, I did see it when you . . .'

'I know, but I thought . . .'

'It's just . . . Sorry to interrupt. I just wanted to say I'd like to come, but I've got to practise that awful *Concerto Ricercante*.'

'Ah, right.'

His jaw goes tense, his shoulders and hands.

'What's the matter? Are you disappointed because . . .?'

'No, but there was one thing,' says Ingmar, blushing slightly. 'I decided just before they made the copy for the premiere to dedicate the film.'

'Who to?'

'Who do you think?'

'Your father,' she teases.

'Stop it.'

'You dedicated *Through a Glass Darkly* to me?'

'Thought you might be pleased.'

'I already was pleased.'

'I don't know, I've never dedicated anything before,' he says quietly.

'Why are you doing it now?'

He lies down on the bed and clasps his hands together on his chest, as he does when going to sleep. Käbi looks at him. Lies down next to him with her head on his shoulder. Tells him he stinks of formalin.

He smiles to himself and starts wiggling his toes.

'This bed's a lot more comfortable than mine, you know – maybe I ought to sleep in here?'

'But separate rooms are more virtuous,' answers Käbi wryly.

'Like at the beginning, you mean? When I crept out of your room . . . at the Palace Hotel, I think it was. I came sneaking out into the corridor in just a dressing gown . . .'

'I remember – wasn't there going to be some sort of press conference?'

'Which we had forgotten.'

She smiles broadly. 'The wrong door opens and out creeps Ingmar Bergman wearing only . . .'

'They did look rather surprised.'

'And what did you say?'

'Guten Rutsch!'

She laughs.

'Well, what else could I come up with? That I'd lost my way? Or was sleepwalking?'

* * *

Ingmar sits at the kitchen table, arranging ham and cheese on a slice of bread. Käbi comes back from the fridge with the jar of mustard.

'All I seem to be able to think about is that you're on your way up to Rättvik,' she says. 'Are you all staying at the Siljansborg hotel?'

'No, only me,' he jokes.

She takes off the lid and pushes the jar towards him.

'Just bear in mind that Ingrid's married to Harry.'

'What are you talking about?'

He takes a knife and spreads a thin layer of Dijon mustard on his ham.

'Only that he presumably won't be as mild-mannered as my poor . . .'

'Käbi? What is it?' he asks softly.

'I do try to believe you when you say . . .'

'Darling?' he interrupts. 'What are you doing?'

'I don't know,' she replies. 'I . . . I just don't understand why you're being so nice. Dedicating a film to me, all that cuddling, looking through old photographs and everything.'

'What do you mean?'

'I'm starting to think you feel sorry for me,' she says. 'Do you? Do you think I've no hope of getting pregnant any more? Is that it? Are you being nice to me because you're on the verge of leaving?'

'What can I do?' he asks. 'What do you want? Promises?'

'No, sorry,' she says. 'I don't mean . . . it's just: I'm under such pressure from Nystroem.'

'Well, why don't you go to Stuttgart?' he says.

'Shall I? I could ring Marialuisa, at any rate,' she smiles. 'I'll do that; maybe she'd have time to come here.'

'Wouldn't it be better if you went to her?'

'Do you want me to?'

It is light and quiet in the Big Studio as Ingmar walks across the floor. Over to the colourless main body of the church. Meets no resistance as he passes through the opening between sheets of chipboard, beams and struts.

Bypassing the porch, he walks under the organ loft and out onto the stone floor of the nave, between the pews.

The rood is hanging from a beam at the entrance

to the choir. It has been moved from the wall to its liturgically correct position. And instead of lofty stained glass, a low window is half-obscured by a tarred altar-screen showing the throne of God.

A nightmarish sensation fills his breast with an unformulated feeling of standing in a burning church. Of the steeply pitched roof and outer walls already being coated in a film of slowly swelling fire. Of the faint crackle heralding a sudden roar as the multicoloured glass in the tall windows whirls into the choir, as the flames gush across the roof to engulf friezes and ribbed vaults.

Only when Ingmar reaches the altar rail does he realize that his strange anxiety is the result of a contradiction: the heat of the spotlights and the dry scent of freshly sawn wood cannot be reconciled with what he sees: that he is in an old stone church.

'We must get going on Gunnel's close-ups,' he mumbles, then shuts his eyes.

Stands unmoving in the warm silence, feels the wave motion running through the whole building, as if it were about to tip forward.

And from the porch, something begins to roll along the aisle towards the altar. There's a rattling like wooden blocks on strings, like slipping hooves on a stone floor.

A spotlight is turned to a new angle with a faint squeak.

Cables are dragged along the pews, get caught on their plinths. Are freed with a quick fling.

A horse snorts and the wooden pew creaks under the weight of a body.

Ingmar opens his eyes and sees Sven discussing something with Peter behind the camera. His eyes tracking the way it is pointing, he turns round.

'How are you feeling?' he asks.

Gunnel is sitting in the pew, breathing through half-open mouth. Her face is swollen, her belly fills out the grey coat. The velvet hat with the ribbon bow is lying beside her.

'Not so bad,' she sighs, and runs her hand over her hip. 'I get a bit of pain here if I walk too fast.'

'How the hell will we get all the close-ups done?'

'I'm not actually giving birth at this moment.'

'Promise?'

Ingmar stops under the archway to the choir, turns with a smile, makes a discreet upward gesture with his hands and says:

'Agnus Dei . . . The congregation will rise.'

Behind Max and Gunnel he glimpses a movement, a ewe's sturdy body, its pale fleece.

Ingmar looks round, looks at Sven. He can feel his hand shaking as he gesticulates in the animal's direction.

'What's up? Do you want her a bit more visible?' Sven queries. 'I thought you wanted her to . . .'

'Can I look through the camera?'

Ingmar trips over the cables, walks round.

Through the system of lenses he can see Max and Gunnel standing in the pew, and diagonally behind them Ingrid, in her light grey sheepskin coat.

'This works,' he says, and goes back to the nave. 'The service is mainly intended as an introduction to the film's characters. Jonas, for example, doesn't help his wife up; his thoughts are elsewhere, as we've said. And Ingrid, you get up the second after. Because you take your lead from them. What I mean is, you're much more like a child in this context, not interested in the ritual.'

Lars-Ove is sitting backwards on a chair, straddling it.

'Good grief, I find it hard to believe in this,' he says, blowing his fringe out of his eyes. 'Starting with a bloody morning service, I mean. It can't be a good idea.'

'Oh, he knows what he's doing,' responds Gunnar.

Ingmar looks away and bites his thumbnail.

'I have been in this business quite a while,' Lars-Ove goes on. 'And I say I don't believe in this – the film's just getting heavier and heavier, and in the end: glug, glug, glug.'

'It's certainly not funny,' sighs Birger.

'Ingmar, tell us it'll be good,' says Gunnar with a smile. 'Of course it'll be good, won't it?'

He shrugs his shoulders and leaves the group.

Paces up and down on the stone floor while the camera is moved for the Holy Communion scene.

Gunnar stands with the chancel arch above him: 'Our Lord Jesus Christ, in the same night that he was betrayed, took bread, and when he had given thanks to God, he broke it and gave it to his disciples, saying, Take, eat, this is my body which is given for you.'

'Good, this is going to be terrific,' says Ingmar, then goes over to Gunnar and lowers his voice a little. 'Bloody good start, right direction and everything, but I don't really want that, what shall I call it . . . fervour. Not that kind of fervour. I mean, it is only a job, after all, and you might not have your thoughts and feelings wholly on it as you stand there in front of the congregation, tired and with a cold and everything.'

'I see,' says Gunnar quietly.

'Priests are best in films,' says Ingmar with a broad smile. 'Aren't they? In real life they never manage to convey the gravity, not the way actors do. Well, maybe my father does. But I think if I'd been a priest the ceremonial would have become more or less like drying the dishes.'

'I'll try to let my mind wander a bit.'

'You just mustn't puff yourself up like . . .'

'I see what you're getting at,' Gunnar stops him in a tired voice and moves away.

Rests his hand on the pulpit.

139

Ingmar looks at him, stops himself from following. He tries to talk to Sven about needing to take down the balustrade of the organ loft for the shots of the organist, while still watching Gunnar.

'Are we ready to roll?' he asks.

The vertical iron girders along the exterior walls of the studio are connected by a framework of thinner strips of metal. Ingmar goes in behind a tall piece of scenery; his hand feels its way along a rusty lath and stops at a junction fastened with steel wire.

He pokes at the plastic between the beams, runs his hand over the protruding roll of yellow fibreglass. Then winds the stiff wire round one of his index fingers, a little too tightly.

He knew Gunnar would react that way, and yet he couldn't stop nagging.

He shuts his eyes and pulls the wire a bit tighter still.

Gunnar's tired face appears, the old words passing across his lips.

Then there is a sort of sighing sound from very close by: a woman drinking something hot.

In the pew next to Märta, the wet-nurse is suddenly sitting with a handkerchief held to her mouth, and Ingmar opens his eyes and tries to take a step back.

He rises from his chair and claps his hands, making the toilet paper he has wrapped round his index finger unwind itself with its recurring pattern of blood.

'That was damned brilliant,' he says. 'A real priest, doing his best, but at the same time stricken by his own human weakness at every moment.'

'I'm not sure.'

'Gunnar, it was perfect,' says Ingmar, giving him a pinch on the arm. 'As usual with you.'

Ingmar sprints over to the group of hands and carpenters.

'What's happening? Don't you need to be getting in there with ladders and stuff? I thought you'd be finished by now. All you've got to do is pull down the bloody balustrade,' he says.

'No, we've got to unscrew it from the inside.'

'Is somebody doing that, then?'

'Jocke.'

'Because I want to get one of the scenes facing the organ done today.'

Lenn holds the door open and then follows him as he strides along the glassed-in corridor.

'Ekelund was on to me this morning, wanting to make sure you know the top limit, because the finance department will only strangle . . .'

'I don't give a shit about them,' he snaps. 'I'm not letting go of this film.'

'Where are you off to?' Lenn asks, laughing.

Ingmar looks amused and indicates the office.

'We've got to get to the Opera House, Ingmar. The meeting's . . .'

'Did I say that?'

'Yes, you wanted to talk through the transport schedule up to Dalarna.'

'Oh yes; when are they loading the editing table?'

'I don't know, but Flodin said the sound bus was ready, at any rate.'

'And the lighting unit?'

'I think Nykvist wants to be there himself.'

Ingmar gets up from his table, swallows his last spoonful of soured milk and walks away. He wipes his hand across his mouth and leaves the canteen.

It makes no difference who it was,' answers Max. 'But he's going round saying you've got scared of . . .'

'Is it Gunnar?'

'Gunnar? No,' says Max, hurrying after him.

Ingmar stops himself running down the steep path. There is frost on the grass, an old thin coating. The sky gleams white above the roof of the silent film studio.

'But I'm no more scared than usual, surely?'

'He says you've started making films for the critics.'

'That explains why they love me.'

'Yes,' laughs Max. 'But seriously, I'm only telling you this because people are getting a bit worried.'

'You as well? Do you think I've lost the knack of creating drama?'

'No, but . . .'

'I can't stage showings just because . . .'

'Though maybe it is time for one now,' interrupts

Max. 'Just so everybody knows you really can, if you want to.'

Coming into Studio Five, they see Allan standing with his coffee mug and a plate with stray crumbs of green marzipan on it.

Gunnar is sucking a spoon and squinting up at the steel girders and gantries in the roof.

'Why the cake?'

'Gunnel's had a daughter,' Allan answers.

'A baby daughter? That's good,' mumbles Ingmar, and stops walking.

He suddenly sees himself shining like a set of new saucepans in the sun. Like a heap of sparkling silver on the ground. Cooking pots, candlesticks, trays and cutlery.

He sits with Ingrid and Gunnar at the editing table, talking about the long take: the teacher's letter to the priest.

'So we're supposed to try to understand her: she's actually, quite simply, desperate.'

'She feels she's about to lose him,' says Ingrid.

'And doesn't grasp the fact that this clinginess is ruining all chances . . .'

He stops himself as Ingrid averts her eyes.

'I don't mean anything bad.'

'No, it . . .'

'Come on, she is a bit revolting with her . . .'

Ingrid gets to her feet; he looks at his watch and tries to change tack.

'We're going to do it straight to camera, but in rehearsals I want you to say it to Gunnar,' he says. 'There's always the risk of losing the feeling or intimacy of another face if you . . .'

'Yes, but . . .'

'No, you're fantastic, you know,' he says hurriedly. 'You both are.'

'As long as I can rehearse until I feel confident,' says Ingrid.

Ingmar is perspiring and takes off his sweater.

'Of course,' he says, and looks at her. 'I don't know if we ought to talk about what happens when she shows her eczema?'

'I'd rather just try out a few things and see.'

'Yes, but bear one thing in mind, Ingrid. This urge for variation, we're leaving all that behind us.'

He laughs and scratches his head.

'Surely we can still try different ideas?'

'But I know I want it simple, pared down,' he answers. 'I've already seen it all.'

'Still, as an actor, you have to,' says Gunnar. 'You have to keep inventing some structure for bits that . . .'

'You two don't need to worry,' interrupts Ingmar. 'You've got it all. All the technical ability and so on . . . But the minute you start believing it's going to turn out boring, it probably will be pretty boring. Don't you think that's how it works, Gunnar?'

'What do you mean?'

'Isn't it only the second-raters who have to resort to a load of technique?'

He laughs. Gunnar gets to his feet and hurls his script aside.

'Gunnar? I didn't mean . . .'

He walks off and Ingmar sits down again.

'Okay, shall I run after him?'

'I think you'd better,' says Ingrid.

He gets to his feet and leaves the studio. Rain verging on wet snow is falling from the dense, deep brown sky. Ingmar walks to the car park, stepping over pools of lying water full of dark autumn leaves, and climbs into his car.

* * *

After their walk along Storgatan in the pale sunlight, as if under a globe of rough-ground glass, they are now sitting at the tea table.

Their eyes are staring into the black room, opening wide onto a stagnant darkness that simultaneously contains a slow rotation of lead-edged plates.

'Did Karin go out to the kitchen?' whispers Käbi.

'I don't know,' replies Ingmar, adjusting the angle of the reading lamp.

A grey gleam passes across his face. His tense jaw muscles are sombrely silhouetted. His dark jacket merges into the blackness of the oil painting on the wall.

Käbi is sitting on one of the eighteenth-century armchairs. She blinks, trying to make out where he is, leans forward and takes his hand.

It is rigid.

Then reacts with a jerk to a sudden crash.

There is a rattle, like metal plates across wood.

Karin has accidentally pulled down the curtain while trying to let in a little of the evening light. She is standing with the dark net in her arms.

'There, isn't that a bit brighter now?' ventures Ingmar.

'Well, perhaps,' says his mother.

Ingmar helps her fold the curtains and sees his father coming from his room with a pale gleam of spun sugar in front of his head.

'Father's got himself a head torch,' says Karin, the corner of her mouth twitching.

With steps that are delicate but not slow, Erik comes right over to Käbi. He is wearing a newly pressed, dark grey suit with a waistcoat and tie.

Only when he comes to a halt does the dim light from the lamp on his brow stabilize. His colourless eyes observe her listlessly. He speaks, holds up his right hand and spreads his fingers wide. Käbi smiles politely and holds up her own hand. Caught at the edge of the light, her fingers gleam like faint yellow filaments.

*

Ingmar walks into a chair, moves it aside, walks on and is just deciding to tell them about the trip to Rättvik tomorrow when the look of his father's mouth changes.

It is no longer a smile.

His forehead flushes red, too. His hand goes to his moustache and then his tie, a little too quickly.

Ingmar approaches him.

Käbi's face flickers briefly into view in the darkness. She has a serious furrow between her eyebrows. And an embarrassed, fractured look to her mouth.

'Did you know we were going to set up a cutting room at Siljansborg?' says Ingmar as he reaches them.

Käbi's hand fumbles for his shoulder.

'Have you been standing there the whole time?' she asks.

'Imagine a lab, a screening room, and all the rest in this sort of setting, a modern editing suite, make-up rooms.'

'Excuse me,' says his father, 'but I have to go and take a telephone call.'

Ingmar follows him.

'Mother told me your birthday went well.'

'I suppose so,' he mumbles.

'The lunch with Agda, I mean, and the outing to the cathedral in the car.'

He opens the door to his study and then turns to Ingmar.

'Was there anything else?'

'No, well only . . . I heard Mother had told you a bit about my film.'

His father sighs and clearly wants to go.

'She thought maybe it reminded you of your time in Forsbacka, Father.'

His breathing is impatient.

'I know this is something quite different,' Ingmar makes haste to add. 'I mean to say, you were well liked at the Works.'

'I think not,' he replies. 'Well liked, that is something else. I was owned, the parish owned me and . . .'

'That's it, that's my thought exactly,' says Ingmar eagerly. 'The priest doesn't belong to himself any longer, I mean, if I'd become a priest, all that would suffocate me: the obligation to do good, the obligation to . . .'

'Though it is rather more complicated than that, in fact.'

'Yes of course, obviously,' he says, beaming. 'But I hope that won't stop you going to see the film, Father, when it . . .'

'I do not intend . . .'

'This is only one aspect.'

'I hardly think your film is the sort of thing for me,' his father says in a kindly voice, before disappearing into his study and closing the door behind him.

148

Ingmar is left standing outside. After a while he gives a cautious knock, but when he receives no answer he goes to the bookcase, feels the backs of the books in the darkness, the cool paper, the smooth leather.

'Ingmar?' calls Käbi softly.

'I'm here.'

She comes over.

'What did he say?' she whispers. 'I realized you were talking about the film . . .'

'Yes, I talked a bit about myself as a priest,' says Ingmar. 'And he thought that sounded interesting.'

'That's great.'

'He said he wanted to see the film.'

'But Ingmar, I heard what he said to you just now.'

'Before that.'

'No,' she whispers.

'Earlier on, Käbi. It's the truth. He said wanted to see the film.'

Karin has cleared away the cups and sugar bowl and is shining a torch into an album of photographs and newspaper cuttings.

'Would you like to see? It's Erik's – keepsake book, I suppose I'd call it, with photos from when Ingmar was growing up.'

Käbi goes towards her, stumbles over something, but regains her balance.

'There's something on the floor,' she says faintly.

'Perhaps it's Erik's briefcase,' says Karin. 'He was looking for it.'

'Felt more like a coat or blanket.'

'Then it can stay there,' she says, shining the torch onto another picture. 'This is Ingmar's twenty-first birthday.'

In a yellow photograph, surrounded by black grass and grey-black fir branches, a group of people is crowded. Ingmar is sitting casually, with neatly combed hair and a high-spirited look, his arm round a woman in a white dress, which has ridden up to reveal her calves. She has been captured pulling a strange face, playfully vengeful, as if she were about to pinch Ingmar in the stomach.

'Who's that?' Käbi asks.

'Marianne von Schantz,' replies Karin. 'And this is Dieter, who lived with us during the war, and Cecilia Thorsell and Nitti.'

Ingmar feels his way to his father's study door.

'Such a serious young man,' says Käbi with warmth in her voice.

'I recall we went to fetch him and some other students in a carriage,' Karin reminisces. 'A team of white horses and . . .'

Ingmar knocks at the door and puts his hand on the handle.

'Lovely picture,' says Käbi quietly. 'I don't know, there's something so nineteenth-century about her, with the hat, and that collar.'

'How Ingmar loved Ma.'

'I know.'

Karin turns the page.

'Laban, my little brother,' she says. 'Folke and Johan.'

'Is that Uncle Johan?'

'And here's little Märta,' says Karin, pointing.

A grey photograph, patterned wallpaper sloping away, and the corner of an oil painting in a gold frame.

Against a highly-polished sideboard where a bunch of lupins and hawthorn droops in a glass vase stands a little boy with a pale, frightened face.

Close to tears, or just after crying.

The boy is dressed in a white shirt and a dark skirt. His bare, bruised legs are thrust at an anxious angle into lace-up shoes with worn toecaps.

Ingmar comes towards the wavering torchlight, to his wife and his mother at the table.

'How incredibly sweet,' says Karin and gives a smile that makes her teeth glint. 'When Putte wet himself he had to wear a red skirt or dress for the rest of the day.'

'I look like a little idiot.'

'No, you look . . .'

They burst out laughing.

'You look like . . .'

'Like an idiot who's peed in his trousers,' grins Ingmar and bites his thumbnail.

Käbi gets to her feet, but can't take her eyes off the picture in the unsteady light.

Sees the boy's protruding ears, his thin, combed hair and fringe cut straight across, before the page is turned.

8

In the darkness, you can make out the hotel from a long way off. First as a flickering clearing among the spruces on the hillside.

Then as a separate entity.

Siljansborg gleams like a transparency in the night.

Next the wooden building grows, with its illuminated verandas, sugar-white mouldings and the shifting light in its rows of latticed windows.

Colossal it rises, with its private reflection onto terraces, steps and frost-whitened gravel forecourt.

A sluggish column of cars and lorries swings round, scraunching, stops and breathes out.

*　*　*

Every morning, twenty-three vehicles leave Rättvik and drive straight into the forest along narrow, dirt roads.

Someone notices that poles from a hay-drying rack have been left there among the brushwood and weeds in the ditch after the harvest. Someone else, perhaps, the hare tracks in the light blue patch of snow behind an uprooted tree.

Or simply the frost in the heather.

The supermarket plastic bag in the low lingon-berry bushes between the pines, or the squirrel stopping in the middle of its vertical rush.

And on one of the first days of filming, just as the straight dirt road enters the tall pine forest, something grabs hold of Ingmar.

Makes his heart beat faster and his hands turn cold.

The clip on his father's trouser-leg. It glitters as the bicycle wobbles.

Then the unpleasant sensation fades and is almost entirely gone by the time they turn off to Finn-backa. The road rises steeply, out of the frosty hollow. Wet pulpwood lies in dismal piles at the entrance to a track used by the timber workers. Muddy tracks left by tractors and trailers, wood trimmings. Splinters and twigs have been dragged onto the track.

In the course of a week, the approach to the red-ochre painted village hall has been ravaged by the heavy vehicles of Svensk Filmindustri. The verges have been churned up by broad tyres; muddy potholes and deep wheel-ruts have been filled more than once with new gravel.

Men are shouting to each other and hauling cables up the wet, grassy slope to the house. A streak of snow

runs along its damp concrete base. A cracked roof tile
stands propped in a cellar window.

* * *

Inside the schoolhouse, Ingmar rests his forehead
against Gunnar's neck, wearily seeking affection.
Then he looks up and says that's roughly how he
visualizes her.

'If you see what I mean.'

He walks off between the desks to show where the
camera is to be placed.

'Because you'll just be two bloody backs to begin
with,' he says. 'And then you'll sit down, Ingrid.'

She nods.

'Do it now.'

She sits down.

'And you don't look at her when you're telling your
lies,' he says. 'And then when you're being so hard on
each other, Gunnar, I want it utterly naked.'

'Which is devastatingly easy,' he jokes.

'I do realize.'

'Well, since you were able to write this in one
morning, I dare say I'll manage to act it.'

'Utterly naked.'

'Of course,' confirms Gunnar.

They smile at each other, but can't help feeling
attacked. Ingrid sits at the harmonium and plays,
while Ingmar stops to look at the children's drawings

on the noticeboard and the light from the stove on the floor.

'By the way, we'll have to have a coal fire tomorrow,' he says. 'Wood's no good, it crackles too much.'

'Too right,' says Stig.

'I'll make a note,' says K.A.

'Shall we run through the whole damn thing now, before we stop?' says Ingmar in a low voice, and they all fall silent and arrange themselves round the walls.

'I'm sick and tired of your short-sightedness,' the priest says calmly. 'Your fumbling hands, your anxiety, your nervous expressions of affection. You force me to pay attention to your physical condition. Your poor digestion, your eczema, your periods, your frozen cheek.'

Suddenly it is as if they are at the theatre, Ingmar realizes. When the audience's entire concentration is absorbed into the actors' portrayals.

Electricians, hands, sound technicians.

Their breathing is shared, the words become their own.

The pale circle in the palm of his hand closes slowly round the glowing pinprick under his big brother's magnifying glass.

The priest grabs the teacher brutally by the arm: 'Can't you be quiet? Can't you leave me alone? Can't you shut up?'

He leaves her at the schoolroom desk and heads out into the hall.

The little audience jostles to make way for him. Tries to let him past and is surprised when he stops and turns round with a smile.

Some of them start chatting in low voices, others find tasks to get on with.

Lennart Nilsson, the photographer from *See* magazine, looks out of the window and pokes gently at the corner of his eye.

Off the corridor by the television lounge at the Siljansberg Hotel, room 605 has been set up as a cutting room: a pale grey steel editing table from Steenbeck & Co., with four turntables and a matte black screen, piles of numbered reels, wrapped for protection in shiny yellow plastic.

The white gloves on Ulla's hands heighten the impression of speed as the film is threaded round little wheels, fed in and wound forward.

Ingmar pulls down the blind and watches as Ingrid's face on the last day at Råsunda appears.

Her look getting more and more pleading.

That voice and trembling mouth.

'Perfect,' he whispers.

'Yes,' says Ulla, and rewinds.

He puts on the light.

'Bugger me, she really is disgusting,' says Ingmar with a laugh. 'No one could love anybody who carries on like that, it's impossible. When she comes out with those demands for affection . . . you just feel like slapping her in the face.'

Ulla says nothing as she changes the reel.

The light is turned out and Gunnar's face comes into view.

Ingmar leans forward.

The priest is listening to the teacher's letter.

The screen goes dark again and Ingmar rubs his chin.

'Isn't it wonderful, Gunnar's face?' he says. 'I mean, it starts off boring, just an actor doing what he's got to do and then suddenly – he fills it from the inside. Makes it more and more naked, exposes all the shame, the whole gamut. That transformation – God-all-bloody-mighty.'

Ulla isn't looking at Ingmar as she rewinds: 'Maybe you should tell Gunnar that sometime.'

'Though he already knows it.'

'If you say so.'

Ingmar is drinking coffee in the library with Gunnar, Max, Ulla and Sven. Replete after dinner, tired after the long working day, they sit in the creaking leather chairs and sofas talking about slips of the tongue and dreams.

Standard lamps with wide, green shades gleam on highly-polished wooden tables, panelling, and old books in glass cases.

'Now it feels good,' says Ingmar, leaning back. 'You know I spent all my summers right here, or in Duvnäs? I remember one morning in June when I went with Father. He was going to preach at Grånäs church. In his summer jacket, with cycle clips on his trousers, a greyish-yellow cravat and a white hat. And I got to sit on the carrier in front, you know. In my bare feet, wearing shorts with blue stripes and a shirt with a collar like this.'

He remembers the trunks of the pines flickering by, suddenly noticing a strange activity between or behind them, like an animation in a zoetrope, a quivering movement inside the slits in the rotating drum.

Ingmar sips his coffee and sees Max's calm eyes. Ulla's mouth, with a bright smile, listening, expectant. And Gunnar, giving him time, looks through the glass doors to the little party of bridge players in the armchairs with the wide-striped cushions.

He carries on describing the landscape of his childhood, but is increasingly disturbed by what is going on behind it. The feeling that something dangerous is approaching.

Fast or slowly, it's hard to say.

More like a twinge of awareness that the descending axe has grazed a twig and changed direction.

He feels he ought to stop his story.

But registers instead that he is adding a thunder cloud to his memory, in an attempt to tackle his uneasiness, to stop it getting the better of him.

He says it was only when they reached the river to catch the ferry that they noticed the brownish purple haycock-towering above the treetops in the middle distance.

'They'd strung steel cables across the flowing water,' he goes on to explain. 'From bank to bank. And the cables ran under rusty little wheels and through iron loops on the ferry. We went on board and Father hung his jacket on a hay-cart. Lined up with the other men and took one of those strange, I don't know the name . . . a kind of gripping tool made of tarred wood. You grabbed the cable with it and pulled the ferry along.'

Ingmar doesn't tell them that his father actually looked feeble and ridiculous alongside the other men. He recalls some of them sneering behind his back.

Unless they were laughing with him, he thinks. His father might have made a joke of it, belittled his own contribution as a way of pre-empting any comments.

The coffee cup rattles in its saucer as some floating timber suddenly bumps the side of the ferry. With a sighing sound, a bluish-grey log is sucked under the flat, shallow hull.

Trembling, Ingmar puts his cup down on the lacquered table, looks up and sees the cables glinting in the morning light against the dark fir forest on the far bank.

Metal scrapes dully against metal and small wheels whine in their housings as he sits down and dips his feet in the cold river. A black surface between two wakes is as smooth as a shop window and the sun suddenly reaches deep down into the water. The cold closes round his ankles in a caressing circle, tugs experimentally downwards, slanting in under the ferry.

'I sat dangling my feet in the water and didn't appreciate how dangerous it was,' Ingmar goes on with a broad smile. 'The heavy logs were bumping the sides, slipping in under the ferry. I was just sitting there splashing when Father grabbed me by the scruff of the neck and hauled me up on deck, gave me a sound telling off and three clips round the ear.'

'You could have drowned,' says Sven.

'But I didn't realize that; I was just angry. I can remember it all in minute detail,' he lies. 'I remember the tools smelled of tar, and Father's forehead was red, and there was a little drop of sweat gleaming on his cheek. And I thought: I'll kill the devil. As soon as I get home I'll devise a painful death for him.'

Ingmar registers Ulla's astonishment and goes on.

'I'll make Father lie on the floor and beg for mercy; I'll shake my head and listen to his screams.'

Max lowers his eyes.

'But the worst thing I actually did,' says Ingmar, 'was to spit in one of his boots, if I remember rightly.'

Ulla laughs and Gunnar smiles and scratches the back of his neck.

The ferry bumped against the bank and dipped; a thin film of water washed across the warm deck.

'I can see why you chose Dalarna for the film,' says Sven. 'Instead of that coastal setting you started out with.'

Ingmar is thinking that in reality it was only one clip round the ear he was given.

His father had hauled him up, boxed his ear and said, his anger severe but controlled: 'Now stand there and behave yourself.'

And then, in everybody's hearing, he had explained that he had been frightened: 'You could have been sucked down and simply vanished.'

Then Ingmar suddenly remembers his own reaction. It had not been one of rancour, as he claimed. But of shame. He felt a failure, sorry for having behaved badly and let his father down. He was afraid of not being allowed to come on future outings. He had been planning to be so good, help in church and win his father's praise.

When they reached the other bank his father gave a slight smile, ruffled his hair and said, 'Come on then, you chump.'

The kindly voice brought tears to Ingmar's eyes; he walked obediently alongside as his father wheeled the bicycle ashore, and bowed to everyone as his father said goodbye.

As soon as they were alone on the road, his father laid the bicycle in the ditch and, cheeks flushed, gripped Ingmar hard by the tops of his arms to give him a good shaking.

Suddenly empty of thoughts, with an absent-minded umbrella motion, Ingmar picks up his cup from the table and drinks some cold coffee. He looks round at the dark panelling, the inlaid woodwork and the spines of the books behind uneven glass.

The actors are talking about their protracted day's work.

'I was on the point of going to spit in somebody's boots,' says Gunnar.

Max and Ulla's laughter dies away as Ingmar spills coffee in his lap.

'Very funny,' he mumbles, looking at his hands and the cup slipping out of them, bouncing off his thigh and landing on the carpet with a chinking sound.

He gets up, stumbles, leaves the library and slams the glass door behind him.

Ingmar goes into his hotel room, shuts and locks the door, rattles the handle and then drags both armchairs over to make a barricade.

*

He sits at the desk, eyes closed, listening to the telephone ringing at the other end. When his mother answers, he has an impulse to hang up at once, but instead he says he wants to speak to his father.

'Was it anything particular?' she asks. 'Because he . . .'

'Yes, it was,' says Ingmar.

'Because he's having a rest on the chaise-longue.'

'Is it his bladder again?'

'He's in pain all the time,' she answers. 'They say he'll have to have an operation.'

'Will he?' murmurs Ingmar, and lapses into silence.

Someone walks slowly along the hotel corridor and stops right outside his door.

'Can't you ring tomorrow instead?'

Small flakes of snow whirl in the light from the window. Other footsteps can be heard in the corridor, lighter than the first ones. This person, too, stops right outside Ingmar's door.

'Ingmar?'

'Yes,' he answers, unstraps his lower leg prosthesis, peels off the sock, looks at the sole of the foot and sees some tiny lettering stamped into the plastic: Össur & Co, Hölzernes Bein ®, he still won't go to see *Winter Light*, Deutsches Erzeugnis 1945.

9

'But I mean, you can't . . . you mustn't push me away. It's incomprehensible how you can be so cruel.'

She sobs, open-mouthed, and a few moments later Ingmar thanks her and calls a halt.

Ingrid dries the tears from her cheeks, wipes her nose with the back of her hand and says she forgot a pause.

'It doesn't matter,' says Ingmar. 'That was good, but I'd like us to do it again, this time with Gunnar.'

Ingmar spins the globe and picks at the seam of the map, which is curling apart at the North Pole.

'All right,' she says quietly.

'I just thought: so you don't forget who you're saying it to.'

She nods.

'Anybody know where Gunnar's got to?'

'No.'

'I do, he's resting upstairs,' says Brian.

'Bugger,' whispers Ingmar, as a whole section of map peels off the globe.

Gunnar comes into the schoolroom with hunched shoulders, clutching a handkerchief.

'How're you feeling?'

'I was trying to get a bit of rest.'

'Ingrid needs some support beside the camera,' says Ingmar. 'Is that okay?'

'Of course,' says Gunnar. 'It's just that I'm not sure I'll be able to cope with my own scenes today.'

'You'll have to try.'

'As long as my voice holds out,' he says, with a less than truthful gesture towards his throat.

'Yes,' says Ingmar, forcing himself not to sound too sharp. 'I know you're worried about your throat, I mean . . .'

Gunnar sits down on a chair, facing Ingrid.

'No, I need you to sit here,' says Ingmar, aware of her tendency to let her gaze wander from the lens hood.

After the take, Ingrid wipes the tears from her cheeks, blows her nose and then spreads the sheepskin coat on the floor between the harmonium and the teacher's desk, among flexes, tripods and boxes of lights.

She lies down and closes her eyes.

Åland and K.A. are standing by her feet, trying to mend the globe with contact adhesive.

Lennart Nilsson climbs up on a desk to take photographs.

Bertha helps Gunnar with his costume, fastens the starched, yellowish collar round his neck.

'Are you running a temperature?'

'Probably,' he mumbles.

'Maybe we should just tuck you up in bed,' says Ingmar. 'I don't know; it's just that we can't afford many more days up here.'

'And with the weather as it is,' says Sven. 'Otherwise we could be getting on with our outside shots.'

Ingmar is standing in the chilly air on the veranda, watching two men in grey boiler-suits moving in the thick mist. They are trying to fasten extra branches on the tree that was planted in the forecourt after the rowan was cut down.

From the porch behind him he can hear an electrician and a carpenter talking about the trade union and comparing subsistence allowances. Their voices sound slightly odd, as if they were pressing their mouths against a cushion.

'It's all just a load of crap,' one of them says suddenly. 'When the money's gone they'll abandon the film, thank you and goodbye, I've seen it all before.'

'But we're talking Ingmar Bergman here,' replies the other one, as if quoting some idiotic slogan.

A woman shouts something, sounding upset, and slams a door. A man swears loudly and then all is silent.

Lights and cameras are being moved, cables repositioned. Sven gestures towards the window and mutters that the mist is far too thick.

'The light'll be wrong,' says Ingmar.

'It won't match the other takes.'

Ingmar perches on the edge of the teacher's desk, idly prodding the globe.

'We'll have to start with close-ups instead, if that's okay,' says Sven.

'Yes.'

'Then we'll need yellow filters up,' says Sven, raising his voice.

Ingmar stands watching while Åland and Håkan fix yellow filters between the outer and inner windows. He bites his nail and stops himself from shouting at them to hurry up.

'Ingrid,' says Ingmar cautiously. 'Wouldn't you like to go upstairs for a rest? I can play opposite Gunnar for you, if you like.'

'I'm sick and tired of your short-sightedness. Your fumbling hands, your anxiety, your tim . . . timid expressions of affection. You force me . . .'

'Cut,' says Ingmar quietly.

'Sorry, I stumbled.'

'Not to worry. In any case, it was a bit . . .'

'Wrong,' says Gunnar.

'It's so important for this scene not to be acted, do you see? For him just to be sitting there with all that hate inside him.'

'You want it to sound like a read-through?'

'No, but you know what I mean.'

'Not sure I do, but I . . .'

'Something's not right here. It's making you get off on the wrong foot.'

'I've no idea what to suggest.'

'Think we'll have Gunnar standing over by the window to start with, instead,' says Ingmar. 'Will that work, Sven?'

'Just need to adjust the lighting slightly.'

'Let's try it.'

The priest leaves his place by the window and suddenly says what he perceives to be the truth.

'Good,' mumbles Ingmar. 'And once you've sat down, Gunnar, just sit there quietly and let the hate come . . .'

'I thought I'd come up with such a good reason. The priest's reputation, I mean. But you dismissed that. I understand you. It was a lie. The real reason is that I don't want you. Do you hear me?'

'Yes, of course I hear you,' supplies Ingmar.

'I'm tired of your solicitude, your fussing, your concerned advice . . .'

'There you go, listing things in your Gunnar way,' Ingmar stops him. 'I don't know. Maybe if you kept your hands in your pockets, you'd have more of that absorption in thought I'm looking for.'

'Hands in pockets. Right.'

'Tell you what? Trial and error,' smiles Ingmar. 'We'll take this scene several times, keep it nice and calm, nice and . . . then maybe we'll do it again later in the week, if we feel we need to.'

'Quiet, quiet.' It goes quiet.

'Take.'

'Camera,' says Ingmar airily.

'Camera rolling,' responds Stig Flodin from the sound control console.

The priest leaves his place at the window, stops, lost in thought.

'I thought I'd come up with such a good reason . . .'

'Cut,' says Ingmar and turns to Sven. 'What's up with the camera? We can't have all that bloody buzzing.'

Gunnar sinks onto a chair and buries his face in his hands.

'Sometimes it makes that noise,' says Sven. 'Sometimes it's . . .'

'But we can't work with it like this,' interrupts Ingmar, and then lowers his voice. 'Can we? It's useless.'

'We'll change the cassette,' says Sven, without meeting his eye.

'Well, hurry it up then,' he answers.

Ingmar goes over to Ingrid, who has come downstairs and is sitting behind the teacher's desk with a coffee cup in her hand. He watches as Sven and Peter work on the camera, scratches his scalp nervously and starts talking about one of the teacher's lines.

'But the priest has just told her the truth,' she says.

'Yes, what he thinks is the truth. Because I don't really believe people tell truths or lies.'

'What do you mean?' she asks with a faint smile.

'Either we can do nothing but lie,' he replies. 'Which means everything we think of as the truth is lies as well.'

'Or?'

'Or the opposite,' he replies good-humouredly.

'That we can do nothing but tell the truth.'

'Because we're actually telling the truth when we lie.'

'I don't understand written words,' sighs Ingrid, in an attempt to concede.

'No actors do,' smiles Ingmar. 'They only understand spoken words.'

'Not those either,' she says with a laugh.

'No, actors are like animals: all they actually do is listen to the tone of voice.'

'I think that's enough,' says Gunnar, getting up from his chair.

Sven and Peter wrap blankets round the camera; they borrow Ingrid's sheepskin coat and spread it over the top.

Ingmar drinks a little water and takes the glass with him as he walks over to Gunnar.

'Do whatever you like this time,' he says. 'I'm almost with Torsten Hammarén when he says he doesn't give a toss what you're all thinking, as long as you've got the voice and the face right. I mean to say, it's the bloody result that counts; as far as I'm concerned you can be thinking rhubarb, as long as it looks good.'

Gunnar looks down at the floor. His jaw is tensed and pale, the line between his eyebrows etched deep.

'Let's try out the camera,' says Ingmar, wiping his palms on his trousers. 'Stand by the window. Go, Sven.'

'Camera,' says Stig.

'Are you filming?' asks Ingmar.

Sven nods.

'Not a sound.'

'Quiet as a knife.'

Ingmar gives a fleeting smile, sits down facing Gunnar and says under his breath that the camera is rolling and he can start.

'I'm sick and tired of your short-sightedness,' the priest explains quietly. 'Your fumbling hands, your anxiety . . .'

'Cut,' says Ingmar, getting to his feet. 'You've got to feel the weight in it. You're simply being honest, after all. And you've got to get away from that alertness. From seeming so articulate. Apart from that, it's spot on.'

'I just don't get this,' says Gunnar without looking at Ingmar. 'I can't do it.'

172

'Don't say that, Gunnar. You're doing it exactly right now, rhythmically and everything. But you're being too alert, you're acting instead of . . .'

'I'm not listening.'

'Come on, I said we were going to do lots of takes,' Ingmar says gently. 'We'll get there in the end.'

'Like training animals,' mutters Gunnar, blows his nose and throws the tissue on the floor.

Ingmar dips two fingers in his glass of water and cools his eyelids. He looks at his watch, drums briefly on the desk and tries to sound affable as he asks if they can put up with a few more takes.

No one answers, but Gunnar goes over to the window.

'Take . . . Camera rolling.'

A log hit the side, the tremor ran through the whole ferry, making the steel cables sing.

And he is hauled backwards, up out of the water, with a grip on his arm and the scruff of his neck, pulled away from the edge and given a clip round the ear that makes everything go black.

'Now stand here and behave yourself.'

He tried to explain that he hadn't got his clothes wet.

'Listen when I'm talking to you,' his father broke in, and then continued more calmly. 'I was frightened. Do you understand? You could have drowned, been sucked under the ferry and simply vanished.'

'I thought I'd come up with such a good reason.

The priest's reputation, I mean. But you dismissed that as a reason. I understand you. It was a lie. The real reason is that I don't want you. Do you hear me?'

'Yes, of course I hear you,' responds Ingmar.

'I'm tired of your solicitude, your fussing, your good advice . . .'

Ingmar remembers the shame he felt at having disappointed his father again. He couldn't understand why he never managed to get it right. He knew full well he had been told to stay by the hay-cart when his father took off his jacket.

They reached the other bank and his father ruffled his hair and said with a slight smile 'Come on then, you chump.'

The kindly voice brought tears to Ingmar's eyes; he walked beside his father, carried his jacket and passed it over once they had reached the road, bowed and said goodbye to everyone, following his father's lead.

A swallow darted like a sudden fracture through the air and disappeared into a hole in the steep, sandy slope.

His father stopped and waited until they were alone, looked round and then rested his bicycle in the ditch, soundlessly in the tall grass. His eyes changed, his cheeks flushed, he gripped Ingmar hard by the tops of his arms, shook him and shouted: 'What do you think? That I enjoy having to watch over you as if you were some snotty brat? Eh? Is that what you think? Let me tell you, Putte, if your mother leaves, I won't care. She can take you with her. And that'll be that. I won't have any children. Do you understand? It's her I love, only her.'

His father righted the bicycle and snapped, 'Stop rubbing your eyes all the time.'

'Sorry,' said Ingmar hastily.

Once Ingmar's father noticed he was following, he mounted the bicycle and pedalled off along the straight dirt road.

'I'm sick and tired of it all,' says the priest. 'Everything to . . .'

'Do that last line again,' Ingmar interrupts, his voice shaking. 'The camera's running. Just start with the whole pause and carry on to the end.'

'I'm sick and tired of it all,' he says quietly. 'Everything to do with you.'

'Why didn't you tell me before? Ingmar asks faintly.

'I was brought up to be polite,' answers the priest, and falls silent.

'Go on, go on,' urges Ingmar, and then looks into eyes that have a new expression.

'I don't give a fuck about this any more,' says Gunnar.

'Like hell,' says Ingmar, running his hand across his mouth.

'I'm quitting, I don't give a fuck about this film.'

'The hell you will!'

Ingmar hurls his water glass straight at the wall. Water and shards of glass spatter the children's drawings and the floor. The metal casing of one of the spotlights gives a hiss.

The room rocks like a raft and a chair falls over as he rushes across.

Gunnar turns away, but Ingmar grabs him by the top of his arm.

'You're not going anywhere,' he screams. 'Do you get it? You're staying here and doing as I tell you!'

He takes his dinner in his hotel room, then switches on the rented television set. The picture comes up gradually, after which Ben Cartwright takes off his hat.

As if he had been standing waiting.

His face is shiny, his grey hair a bit tousled.

The line just above the bridge of his nose, between his black eyebrows, leads Ingmar to fantasize about a large, false nose.

'Who do you think you're fooling, Putte?'

Ben takes off his false nose and puts it down on the Bible, mutters the question again and wipes his index finger under his snotty little snub nose.

Ingmar feels embarrassed.

Ben leans forward, close to the screen, as if looking in a mirror. And as he starts to detach his attractive top lip, Ingmar turns off the television.

*

He remembers that he picked up the letter his parents had left lying on the table and stood alone in the dining room to read what Dag had written. It was only his second winter month as a volunteer at the Front in Finland. He had frostbite on both ears and one foot, but claimed he was well.

You're lying, Ingmar had thought.

Dag wrote that he hadn't anything particular to tell them, though they all knew the Swedish unit had got caught in the air bombardments of Kemijärvi.

'Because I shan't say anything about the war,' Dag wrote.

The whole point of the short, reserved letter was to get his parents to send him some milk chocolate and a helmet cover.

'I've brought some chocolate,' says Ingmar, knocking on the door.

At the other end of the hotel corridor, at the foot of the stairs, the bracket lamp on the wall casts a strong, hazy light across the red-medallioned wallpaper.

Ingmar stands there for a while, looks at the box of chocolates and then knocks tentatively.

Faint squeakings run jerkily across the ceiling.

'Gunnar?' he says in a low voice, and knocks again.

He closes his eyes and one hand finds its way to his stomach, eases the pressure of his trouser waistband for a moment.

Radio music is audible but then dies away. A piano piece, falling soporifically.

'We need to talk,' he says, though he does not knock again.

Slowly he sets off down the corridor, hearing the

wooden floor beneath the carpet respond to his weight.

There is someone moving beyond the blinding glare of the wall lamp, hidden by the white light.

A thin leg, a crutch.

Ingmar approaches, but suddenly turns and starts walking in the opposite direction, breaks into a run, takes the stairs up to the next floor with great strides. He catches his foot on the top step.

His heart is beating fast by the time he stops outside the doors of the television lounge. He tries to tell himself that he can't have seen the wet-nurse from the apartment awaiting demolition, that it must have been somebody else. He waits a bit, runs a hand over his hair, knows he must calm down. Find his way out to his proper face. To his mouth and eyes.

Light blooms sporadically against the opal-glass.

March music blares abruptly from a tinny loudspeaker.

Then it goes dark. And soon after, quiet.

Ingmar steps forward and knocks on the door, opens it and looks inside. He feels for the switch and turns it. The chandelier trembles, but then – at the far end of the room – a dim table lamp in the shape of a beggar boy clutching an accordion to his chest comes on instead.

Ingmar enters and tries to look cheerful as he realizes everyone is hiding from him. They are wedged behind the green sofas, the long curtains, the writing desk and the television cabinet.

But as if he had simply not noticed that they were playing a joke on him, or as if he saw nothing strange in Ingrid crouching on all fours behind an armchair, or Max lurking between the window and the curtain, he started telling them about his dream.

'I was about to direct a Strindberg play at the Royal Dramatic Theatre,' he says, and sits down on the sofa. 'The set design was hideous: some scraggy cherry trees and real water pipes, running like this.'

The television cabinet creaks, there's a shuffling at the back of the sofa, and suddenly he feels something nuzzle his ankle and looks down. A ewe is resting her head on the floor, her moist nose just by his foot.

'The schedule began with a rehearsal for the extras,' Ingmar continues, seeing the horse lift its head and toss it to one side to shake off the lace curtain.

'I was going to tell them what the play was about, and asked them to be quiet. But they all went on talking as if I wasn't there. They were playing with an old fishing rod they'd found, laughing.'

A heifer, her tether dangling, emerges slowly and with gravity from her hiding place behind the writing desk. The light of the table lamp sheds an oily glimmer on her light brown hide.

'I told them this was the only Strindberg play that has to be done with complete realism. But when the extras just went on talking and messing about, I had a little fit of rage and roared: Rehearsal over.'

He leans down and pats the sheep's woolly cheek. She screws up her eye, turns round, scrabbles the air with her hooves, falls over heavily on her side and gets up again, snorts, and moves off down the side of the coffee table.

The heifer opens the door to the corridor with her muzzle, squeezes her head through and pushes her way out. The self-closing door slides over her shoulders, along her smooth flank and catches briefly on her pelvic bone.

The horse leaves the television lounge after her with heavy steps, his head hanging.

Then the ewe, with great dignity. Earth and straw in her fleece. Followed by a grey-black pig with luminous eyes.

Ingmar remains on the sofa, alone. It has all gone quiet in the corridor. The beggar boy casts a pale gleam on panelling and console tables: the jaw area lets through the most light, while the accordion spreads only a brownish glow.

The antimacassar falls down behind the sofa when Ingmar gets up and goes over to the window; he undoes both catches and opens it into the darkness.

Deep down in black water, the stars flutter.

He climbs up into the narrow window recess, holds on tight with one hand round the post in the middle and the other on the curved lintel at the top, leans out into the cold air. Maybe eight metres above the frozen slope, and feels a melancholy calm spread through his body.

Flaking paint falls onto the windowsill.

His heart beats its heavy, sinking beats.

He loses the feeling in his hands, contact with his feet, is hanging right out of the window and could almost imperceptibly let go.

The front of the hotel, rows of mute windows, the delicate fretwork and the terrace far below, with accumulations of autumn leaves and snow.

A pine casts its threadlike moonshadow; four stars lie across the others like an arrow; solitary lights are faintly visible in the valley and the vast lake seems darker than the sky.

10

Ingmar does not dare open the letter, afraid that it will be about his father. His condition is worsening by the day. The operation will have to be retimed; Nanna Svartz is involved now.

Ingmar sees Stig outside the breakfast room and says he thought they could take the last shots in Skattunge church and perhaps start looking at the settings round the suicide site.

'I thought it was all off.'

The hand holding the letter suddenly jerks, as spasmodic as a daddy-long-legs.

'Why would it all be off?'

'Ekelund rang and said . . .'

'What the hell's he got to do with it? Sorry, but wouldn't it be better to talk to me?'

Stig has his hand over his mouth the whole time he is talking. He looks sceptical: 'Were you planning to film today?'

'Yes.'

'Thing is, I gave my lads the day off.'

Ingmar thrusts his hands into his trouser pockets and looks Stig in the eye.

'Can you try to get hold of them?'

'Yes, but . . .'

'Try,' says Ingmar, and starts walking away.

He turns in the doorway, sees Stig's departing back and calls, 'We've got to work today if we're going to pull this off.'

Ingmar goes on into the breakfast room and stops as his thoughts return to his fury with Gunnar, to the second the glass smashed against the wall.

Sharp splinters and round droplets.

He moves slowly sideways, looking at the sparse sunburst of glass shards and water. Sees the children's drawings reflected thousandfold within its orb.

And Gunnar's frightened eyes vaguely discernible through this transient crystal chandelier.

Ingmar moves a little further and Gunnar's face disappears, materializes again and is then erased as the angle fills the water droplets with the glare of a spotlight. He stands on tiptoe, bends his knees and sees someone else beside the spot where Gunnar should be standing.

It is a child. Stefan perhaps, thinks Ingmar.

A boy trying to hit somebody but not reaching. He is being restrained by a rigid arm. A hand flat against his forehead, gripping him by the hair.

Ingmar goes over to the actors, puts his cup of tea on the table and sits down.

'So you all think we're having a day off today?'

'Gunnar is ill, you know,' says Ingrid irritably.

'I only meant . . .'

'Well, what did you mean, then?' she interrupts.

'Nothing.'

'Because I've got a bit of a sore throat too,' she says. 'But maybe I'm just putting it on.'

He looks down into his tea. A ripple runs across its dark surface.

'I just wanted to know if you'd be prepared to come to Skattungbyn?'

'Of course,' replies Max, looks at the others and shrugs.

Katinka comes into the breakfast room and beckons Ingmar over.

K.A catches him up in the corridor, mumbles that he's worried and does up the button on one of his shirt cuffs.

'Have you spoken to Gunnar?'

'I was just on my way,' answers Ingmar.

'Don't think you'll get him out to Finnbacka again.'

'No, I wouldn't dare suggest it,' says Ingmar, smiling. 'I hope we'll be able to edit together what we've got.'

A wall-mounted telephone rings.

'I don't know,' says Stig with a dejected look. 'People seem totally . . . almost as if they didn't believe there would be any film. Nothing works if everyone goes round thinking like that.'

'No.'

'Ingmar,' says Stig, trying to catch his eye. 'How are things looking, really? How many days can we stay?'

'I don't honestly know,' he replies, pressing himself against the side of the glass jar.

The telephone rings again.

'You really ought to speak to the boss – if only the sun stops shining, we'll be done in about a week.'

'We could do the lot in four days,' says Ingmar. 'And we've got the money for that, but I mean, we seem to have lost today, and if Gunnar's not well enough to work tomorrow we might as well go home.'

K.A.'s mouth begins to tremble.

'It'll work out,' says Ingmar gently.

K.A. just stands looking at him.

'Would you mind seeing if you can find Blomquist and his gang, then we can take a little drive and look at the suicide site today.'

Ingmar sees Britt Arpi through the glass doors to the reception area. Turns away at the very moment her mouth is widening. 'Bergman,' he hears behinds his back.

He breaks into a run so he won't have to hear her mention the telegram that came that morning.

He goes swiftly along the corridor.

He comes up against a wall of glass, turns a somersault and flutters backwards up to the ceiling, is bounced from there into the glass shade and burns himself on the light bulb, lurches to the floor, flies round the corner, carries on down half a flight of stairs and then starts walking.

Stops, looks at his watch for no reason, goes a little further and knocks warily on the door.

'Who is it?'

Ingmar opens the door and sees Gunnar lying in bed, reading.

His book sinks onto his chest and he shuts his eyes.

'I thought I'd look in on you.'

'Well this is how I look,' he mutters.

'Is your throat sore?'

'I can't work today.'

'I realize that,' says Ingmar quickly. 'But what do you think about tomorrow?'

Gunnar does not reply.

'Because I'm afraid we'll run out of money if we . . . there's nothing to be done about it, but . . .'

Gunnar opens his eyes, his lips tighten and turn even paler.

'Do you want a get well card?' asks Ingmar, and can't stop himself smiling. 'Father showed me a greetings card I drew for my grandmother when I was about six, I think. It's covered in red and yellow faces and a mass of dots. On the back my mother wrote, "The picture apparently shows everything on fire".'

Gunnar goes back to his book.

'This is actually the first time my father has wanted to see a film; I even had to promise him it would get made,' he lies.

A car horn beeps outside, a lazy fanfare. When Ingmar pulls aside the curtain and looks down onto the gravelled forecourt, an unknown man in front of a black car gives an expansive wave.

Ingmar sees Sven standing waiting in the corridor outside his room, head hanging. His sandy hair is tousled and his sugar-rimmed eyes look tired.

'What is it?' Ingmar enquires. 'You look totally . . . I don't know. Things will sort themselves out, it's always like this.'

'It's just that the lab has reported a defect.'

'Which take?'

'They're not sure whether it really is anything, but . . .'

'Is it Gunnar's scenes? It is, isn't it?' asks Ingmar. 'Well now we've had it, come what may.'

Sven lowers his eyes and a flush colours his cheeks and the skin around his pale eyebrows. Ingmar doesn't know what to say, hasn't the energy to continue the conversation, is too tired to sound positive. He unlocks his door, leaving Sven in the corridor, shuts it gently behind him and lies down on his stomach on the bed.

The telephone line crackles, occasionally chopping up their voices, and the conversation is surrounded by a dreamlike sensation of some kind of drifting, falling.

'No, I got back the day before yesterday.'

'How did it go with Marialuisa?'

'She is as she is,' says Käbi. '*Nur Ruhe.* She split everything into its component parts; conjured up a conductor who taught himself the orchestral score from the piano arrangement.'

A pipe gurgles somewhere.

'And on . . . Sunday, it was, she persuaded a shop that sells grand pianos to let us in,' Käbi goes on. 'Invited along loads of her students and friends.'

'Did it go well?'

'I felt I was on top of it, at any rate.'

'There you are, then,' says Ingmar.

'How about you?' she asks. 'You sound a bit down.'

'I don't know . . .'

'Has something happened?'

There is a faint clicking in the silence and a buzz of other voices echoes briefly in the background. Käbi takes a breath and her voice is unsteady as she goes on.

'Have you done it now? Have you met somebody?'

'What?' he asks in surprise. 'Give it a rest; I'm having all sorts of problems with the film.'

'Just say if you've met somebody. You know you can tell me about it. I'm not the jealous type, but I don't want you to lie.'

'Käbi, I haven't met anybody.'

'But you're sleeping with Ingrid?'

'No, just the opposite, you might say.'

'You're sleeping with Gunnar?' she says with a smile.

He laughs and says perhaps he ought to try that.

'Have you fallen out with each other?' she asks, still sounding amused.

'I lost my temper yesterday and started shouting,' he says. 'And Gunnar decided he'd had enough and went off sick.'

'As long as you'll have time to get finished.'

'Well, it doesn't look like it,' he says softly. 'There might not be a film after all.'

'Seriously?'

'Well, I don't know, but the money's nearly all gone and everyone just seems so tired and fed up.'

'But of course there's money.'

'It's just, it probably was stupid of me to insist . . .'

'But this is an important film,' Käbi says.

'Well of course I want to show Father that I . . .'

'I mean for you, important for you, for yourself,' she interjects. 'After all, he won't see the film when it comes to it.'

'Oh, I think he will.'

'Okay,' she murmurs.

The line crackles.

'What?'

'And do you think he'll approve of it?' she asks.

'He'll say I don't know anything about priests,'

answers Ingmar with the beginning of a smile.

Once he noticed his son was running after him, Father had swiftly mounted his bicycle, wobbled once and started pedalling. Off along the straight dirt road, crossing boundary lines and overgrown timber tracks.

Ingmar can see the tails of the thin jacket fluttering over the bag on the back carrier.

And the little boy running after his father as fast as he possibly could, and his father arching his back and pedalling faster.

Straight into the shadowy blue channel through the pines.

'Well, you'll have to talk to Gunnar, to all of them,' says Käbi, 'and say you're sorry for getting so angry.'

'But I can't face it,' he replies. 'Just want to sit here watching TV.'

'But the film will . . .'

'Besides, there's a Saturday night dance in the hotel,' he says. 'And I bet everyone will be there by now.'

'Go and join them, then.'

'I can't stand dances,' he giggles.

'You don't need to dance, you know, just because . . .'

'I can't, Käbi. I'm so desperate, I'd burst into tears.'

'Well do that, then,' she suggests.

'Yes,' he smiles, feeling a tightening, high up in his nasal cavity. 'That would be something.'

11

Ingmar is staying with his father at the main hotel in Söderhamn. After lunch, they catch the train to Bergvik and go to the cinema.

Harold Lloyd.

From the very back of the auditorium comes a sudden knock at the door.

Not a hard one, but Ingmar is still impelled to open his eyes.

He sees the morning light on the ceiling. The electric light off, the glass shade with dead flies in the bottom.

There is another knock and he gets out of bed, shifts aside the two armchairs and opens the door,

Sven eyes him with cautious relief and comes into the room. K.A. follows, carrying a small breakfast tray.

'I just got hold of the lab,' says Sven. 'And there's no problem, it was . . .'

He beams and then stares at the floor.

'It was just some nonsense,' he goes on. 'It all looks perfect, they said.'

'That's good,' mumbles Ingmar.

'We can view it this evening.'

K.A puts the tray on the bedside table.

'And I had a word with Ingrid and Max at breakfast,' he says. 'They say Gunnar seems better today.'

'That's nice for him,' says Ingmar, getting back into bed.

'Is anything up?' asks Sven.

'What's up is that nobody wants to make this film except me . . . and even I don't know any more.'

K.A. goes over to Ingmar's window; a moment later he mutters: 'Stig and his lot are already out there.'

'What's the weather like?' Ingmar asks.

'It's sunny, but looking in that direction I'd say it might cloud over soon, with any luck.'

'I suppose I'd better get dressed, then,' says Ingmar.

Stig is standing in the foyer, talking about a special pipe he's whittling out of pear wood.

'I do a bit each day.'

Gunnar and K.A. carefully unwrap the chamois leather on the glass table.

'For two fills,' says Stig, scanning their eyes for a reaction. 'Either the same tobacco in both, or two different kinds.'

They study the pipe like experts. Hold it up to the electric light.

'For two fills,' repeats Gunnar with concealed mirth.

'This one's more like a sidecar,' says K.A.

When Ingmar comes over, Gunnar passes him the pipe.

'Does it work?' he asks in a low voice.

'Work?' echoes Stig. 'How do you mean?'

K.A. laughs and turns his face away, and Ingmar can see Gunnar's eyes sparkling as he hides his mouth with his hand and sits down on a chair.

Sven comes in with the cold air in his clothes.

'Rats got into the car. They've eaten half the stuffing,' he pants. 'Why did it have to be my seat? Huge holes all over.'

'Maybe it smells tasty,' says Ingmar, rubbing himself against the doorpost to scratch between his shoulders.

'Smells tasty?' mutters Sven. 'You don't have to eat everything that . . .'

'I was joking, Sven.'

'You think it smells bad?'

Ingmar laughs and Sven looks happy as their eyes meet.

'Shall we head for Skattungbyn?'

'I really don't know,' says Ingmar.

'We've still just about got time.'

'If we ignore the bloody sun, ignore the bloody . . .'

'We won't ignore anything,' interrupts Sven. 'It'll be perfect, that's what it'll be.'

In the dazzling light, Skattungbyn dominates the steep hillside above the road as they continue down into the valley.

The convoy of cars and trucks turns off along a smaller, unmade road, makes its way through the forest as the surrounding mountains close around it.

They slowly wind their way along the shores of the glittering system of lakes.

The heavy vehicles, the sound unit and the canteen stop at the entrance to a gravel pit, opposite the turning place. The outflow from the last lake foams and gushes from an open sluice-gate, down into Marnäs River.

'I like it,' says Sven, advancing from the car. 'That's good.'

He points at the dam.

Ingmar nods.

'Even if there aren't that many steamers just here,' says Katinka, smiles broadly and tries to catch Ingmar's eye.

They are all going round wearing the same jackets, with sheepskin linings. They stand stamping in the sunshine on the gravelled area to keep warm.

Two-year-old birches quiver among the coppice shoots. Fall silently or remain hanging.

'Blomquist's got permission to chop down some of the bushes by the falls,' says Sven, mainly to himself.

He stands alongside Ingmar for a minute and then goes down to Peter, who is setting up an insulated camera on a wooden platform.

K.A. walks over to Ingmar and points to the wet

canopy of clouds pressing in over the treetops, without saying anything.

Ingmar gathers them round the camera, but stands in silence for a long time, not knowing what to say.

'This doesn't feel very . . . easy, for want of a better word,' begins Ingmar. 'But my idea for today was to do all the takes from a distance. What I wrote in my own script was that we must never get too intimate with the dead body and . . .'

The actors and technicians are ranged in front of him.

'I know it's my fault we've lost so much time.'

He takes off his cap and scratches his forehead.

'And if the sun carries on shining, well . . . I don't know, we'll just have to make some huge compromises, do lots of close-ups and park the trucks close to give us a bit of shadow, but . . . What can I say? This is really me, on the verge of failing to hold the service. You do what you want. No one's obliged to stay, but I hope most of you will let me have a couple more hours.'

Ingmar is pointing and shouting as they rehearse the big set-pieces. Cars drive up, turn round.

The priest strides forward, stops.

Exchanges a few inaudible words with the plain clothes policeman.

An old tarpaulin is spread over the body.

*

Sven goes down to where Ingmar is standing and reminds him the ambulance mustn't back too far.

'This would have been good – wouldn't it?' says Ingmar.

'Yes.'

'Damn good, I bet.'

'I can almost persuade myself it's clouding over a touch,' says Sven, and sniffs to stop his nose running. 'And it really is colder; in this last hour it's got . . .'

'I thought that, too,' says Peter, passing a notepad to Sven.

'Yes, if only we could have a bit of snow as well,' responds Ingmar quietly.

'But I think maybe we should hurry up and get filming,' says Sven. 'Before the sun comes out again.'

'No, we'll have lunch now,' mumbles Ingmar, looking down to the water.

The spruce forest has turned greener, he thinks, and suddenly he sees blackness rising up from the dull mass. Then washing softly outwards and spreading like a pale grey film along the ground and away over the lake.

He carries his deep plate of steaming beef stew carefully round tables and chairs. The floor shakes and thunders under his feet. The windows are covered in condensation. He takes the seat opposite Gunnar. They look at each other and then eat in silence.

*

Ingmar closes his thick jacket over his chest, pulls the belt tight round his waist and sees the first snowflakes against an inky blue spruce; he realizes how dark it has gone, looks up at the roof of cloud that has closed over the filming location and the light snow whirling round in the squally wind.

'Not bad at all,' says Ingmar, and then shouts 'Hurry up now – we're shooting.'

Sven emerges, sandwich in hand.

'Incredible.'

'Bloody beautiful.'

'Places please.'

'Get those cars out of here.'

Ingrid is laughing as Bertha checks her costume and adjusts her hair.

'Those cars have got to go.'

'Here comes the blood,' sings Börje, running alongside K.A. clutching a five-litre purple bottle in his arms.

Ingmar climbs up onto the wooden platform, stands beside Sven and watches the snowflakes swooping in the wind across the turning place, the shiny car roof and the corpse under the tree.

'This is what we've been waiting for.'

'I know,' says Ingmar calmly.

A car pulls up in front of the ruffled, dammed-up surface of the water. The priest walks quickly, passes behind a black car with muddy sides.

Just beyond the base of the bridge over the dam, two men are waiting, a few steps from the lifeless body.

Snow eddies in the wind, just above the ground.

The priest covers the last stretch more slowly.

When the second take is finished, when Gunnar has been sitting in the car beside Ingrid for a minute, Ingmar claps his hands.

And before they have even had a chance to discuss filming some reserve shots, the snow stops.

The sky is emptied to the last flake and rises into renewed solitude.

It grows a little lighter, and by the time Ingmar gets down to Gunnar, the sun is breaking through over the white surfaces of the water in the network of lakes.

'Looked good,' says Ingmar.

'Thanks,' says Gunnar gruffly.

They stand contemplating the turning place, the tyre tracks and the snowflakes still tumbling along the ground.

'Shall we try to finish this film?' asks Gunnar.

'Perhaps we should,' he answers.

'In that case, we really ought to see if we can get the inside shots at Skattunge church done today,' says Gunnar.

'That would be bloody good,' replies Ingmar.

'Well this is hardly the time to hang about here sulking, then.'

'Hardly,' echoes Ingmar.

They exchange a brief smile and start walking towards the others.

12

Ingmar is forced down onto his right knee. Tugs at his frozen shoelace, trying to undo a reluctant bow.

Käbi comes into the faint darkness of the hall.

Without saying anything, she goes up to him, and staggers slightly as he puts his arms round her legs.

He presses his cool face against her abdomen.

'You see, I could get pregnant, after all,' she whispers, and starts stroking his head; her fingers comb aimlessly through his hair.

Via his skull he can hear the movement, like sand, across his scalp.

And distantly, a cello answering a vanished piano. A gentle mazurka from the radio or gramophone. Languid, as if suspended in sugar syrup, a diminuendo.

They stay just as they are, forgotten.

Then he hears her intake of breath.

'What do you think?'

'That you're very clever,' he answers.

Her whole face lights up in a smile.

'Well yes, I am rather clever, aren't I?'

He stands up.

'But are you prepared for this?' she asks.

The light from the next room illuminates the half of her face that is turned away. In the hall mirror he can see her cheeks flush.

'Are you happy?' she asks.

He nods.

'And you?'

'So happy I . . .' she says, cautiously dabbing under her eyes. 'So happy I feel ashamed. I think about Linda and I'm ashamed of . . .'

The words stick in her throat and she leaves the hall, her hand over her mouth.

In a glass jar with a screw lid there is a little stage of painted cardboard, with a forest green backdrop and a raised curtain.

Ingmar bounces nervously on the pale blue, miniature sofa.

A dressing room door opens and out comes Käbi in a white slip and beige bra.

'Did you find time to visit your father this morning?' she asks.

'No, I . . . well, finding the time isn't the issue. You know I don't like hospitals,' he says, his mouth twitching. 'And I don't like sick people. Can't bear them. The way they lie there, looking at you. In their nightshirts. With tubes and plasters . . .'

'It isn't funny.'

He belches from the stress of it all, flaps his hand in front of his mouth and starts rocking on the sofa.

The telephone rings, sounding muffled, as if under a blanket.

Ingmar gets up and reaches to put the glass jar on a shelf, but misses. It topples over the back of his hand and falls on the floor.

Like breaking a dry twig across your knee, there is a sudden snap. And instantly the shards lie scattered across the carpet.

The telephone is still ringing; Ingmar hastily picks his way through the glittering fragments, goes into his study and answers.

He sits at the desk, looking out over the garden, the snow-covered branches in the darkness, while he tells his mother that he met Greta Garbo on Thursday. He describes her calm, chipped voice. And he tells a little lie about her inquisitive gaze reminding him of his mother's.

But she does not laugh, or brush his comments aside.

Instead, it all goes quiet.

Nothing but the wheezing of the telephone line.

A branch against the windowsill.

'Is anything the matter?' he asks.

'Father's worse.'

Ingmar knocks over the empty mineral water bottle as he reaches for the packet of biscuits.

'Worse? How do you mean, worse?' he asks, then lowers his voice. 'The operation went well. Why the hell should he be worse?'

With a shaking hand he breaks off a little bit of biscuit and puts it in his mouth.

'They said something about complications, I don't know, I . . .'

'What sort of complications? Didn't they say? You'll have to ask what the complications are. We need to know how he is, don't we? I mean, think if he's in a bad way, just think if he's in a really bad way.'

'Ingmar, all they said was that he was worse.'

'Then ring and ask what they mean by worse.'

'But I've only just . . .'

'Ring again,' he screams, and hangs up.

Käbi knocks and comes in. Stops behind him. Reflected in the window, she stands there. A dark figure, pierced by branches, encircled by yellow light.

'Your mother, I gather,' she says in an unruffled voice.

The falling snow thickens; sheets of interlinked snowflakes sail heavily down.

'Had she been to the hospital?'

He nods.

'How was he?'

'Oh, he'll be all right,' murmurs Ingmar.

'But Karin wanted you to go and see him? Went on about . . .'

'No,' he says.

'So what is it?'

206

'Nothing,' he says, getting to his feet. 'Or, I don't know, I'm making a film about people suffering, dying.'

'What's the matter?' she asks, raising her voice.

'Nothing. It's just that Father's worse.'

'Is that what the doctors say?'

'Yes.'

'Then I think you should go to the hospital.'

The telephone rings and Ingmar's face tenses; his lips turn pale.

'It'll be Mother,' he says quietly.

In the light from the kitchen he sees a magpie stalk across the deep snow to the greeny-black ring round the cherry tree and start to peck the ground.

The telephone rings again.

'You know you don't have to answer.'

'I must just get . . . Ow, flaming hell.'

'What is it?'

'I trod on . . .'

'A piece of glass?'

'I don't know . . .'

He picks up the receiver, puts it to his ear and mumbles his name.

'They let me speak to a doctor,' his mother tells him. 'Father's got another infection and his temperature's very high. That was all he could tell me.'

'But what does a very high temperature mean?'

'You could always go over there and . . .'

'I'm in the middle of editing a film.'

Käbi takes off his sock, switches on the desk lamp and props up his foot.

'Every day I sit with him,' says Karin. 'Sometimes I stay the night and sleep on the couch, but you can't even find time for one visit.'

Käbi peers closely, lightly presses the sole of his foot. Her fingertips are bloody as she adjusts the angle of the lamp.

'There's no point disturbing Father just because I'm worried.'

Käbi investigates cautiously with her fingernail.

'Don't talk to me about worry,' his mother says severely. 'If you were the least bit worried, you'd be at his bedside.'

Käbi gets up and places something on the table in front of him.

'That won't make him any better,' replies Ingmar, and suddenly feels his breathing inhibited by an advancing series of cramps.

'How can you be so cold?'

He picks up the little splinter of glass, tries to get to his feet, has to lean against the wall for support and hears himself whisper:

'You mustn't say that.'

'Why mustn't I?'

'He'll only be disappointed when he sees it's me visiting him.'

The piece of pink glass is shaped like a little pocket mirror with a tapering handle.

'Don't try to make excuses,' she says with a smile in her voice. 'You don't care about him. Be honest. The only thing you . . .'

Käbi takes the receiver from Ingmar and hangs up. He just stands there, staring blindly out over the room.

* * *

She stops at the foot end of the bed with the magnifying glass in her hand; the shadow she creates lies there on the carpet.

'Try to think about something else,' she says.

Ingmar sits with his head hanging and his hands squeezed together between his thighs.

'He can't die of a high temperature.'

'Did they say there was a risk he might?' she asks.

'I don't know, I don't know anything.'

'We could go there together and just . . .'

'Käbi,' he cuts in. 'I don't think I can do it.'

She puts the magnifying glass on the bedside table.

'Thanks,' he says.

'It was in the bottom drawer.'

He holds the magnifier over the splinter of glass. From one angle it really does look like a pocket mirror, or a magnifying glass, but in place of the mirror glass or lens you can, with a little imagination, make out a sort of engraving.

Two little matchstick men, maybe. But if that's what they are, one of them has no arms.

And the bigger one has a stalk growing out of his shrivelled head.

'You probably shouldn't leave it too long if there's anything you need to say to him,' she says quietly.

'Eh?' whispers Ingmar.

The magnifying glass trembles in his hand.

'What are you doing?' asks Käbi.

The other matchstick man seems to be tilting his head back.

Perhaps he's laughing, his cheeks red with clotted blood.

Yet the next moment his voice is very earnest as he explains that it's different for him, because he has never been able to talk to his father.

'No, I'm the one who can't do that,' says Ingmar.

'What?' asks Käbi. 'What can't you do?'

'I make films, and now . . .'

'But he couldn't care less about them,' shrieks the matchstick man with the stalk on his head.

'It's different this time,' Ingmar retorts.

He sings Baba's judgment on the man in the car, out on the dark roads, pops a chocolate coin in his mouth and beats time on the steering wheel.

Despite always driving a little too fast, he never manages to get more than the bonnet of the car into the rotating cylinder of snowflakes.

A road sign glides up to the whirling top and carries on round, like a gondola on a giant Ferris wheel.

The bed canopy of the sky rises at Slussen before closing round the custom house and the barges along the quays at Stadsgårdshamnen. As if viewed through mosquito screens, the channels through the ice over to Kastellholmen and Djurgården are a blur.

He turns into Folkungagatan and parks outside Ersta Hospital, sits in the car with the engine ticking over, regarding the big building of pale yellow brick through the falling snow.

The pointed tin roof and the rows of windows decorated with advent stars.

Patches of condensation spread across the windscreen, two blind eyes joining together.

A faint rustling sound runs beneath the car.

Stops and begins again.

Through the ever denser grey of the windows, Ingmar can just make out a door opening at the main entrance.

A little too slowly.

And to begin with, there is nothing to be seen; then a small, black body squeezes out.

A human figure on all fours.

Or a goat, he thinks, and sees the vague shape of twisted horns and narrow, floppy ears.

It could be a goat standing outside the entrance by the granite plinth, nodding in his direction.

It raises its wispily bearded chin and he waves back, tentatively.

The goat stamps its right hoof.

Ingmar wonders if it is summoning him, and the goat nods impatiently.

It turns round, gives a shiver that runs the length of its back, and does something with its front feet that he can't see.

Ingmar wipes the steamed-up windscreen, but now the space outside the main door is empty.

The big panes of glass in the door shake and then are mute.

Ingmar gets out of the car and realizes he has driven from Djursholm without his jacket or wallet. He stands in the cold air in trousers and shirtsleeves. Weightless snow whirls along the ground, collecting in dunes against walls and round traffic islands.

Ingmar skirts the side wing, continues along by the old main building with its yellow plastered front, peers in through the windows with a hunted look, but can see no wards with patients.

He warms his hands under his arms for a while, then climbs up onto an electrical box and looks into a little room.

Unwieldy pieces of equipment cover the walls, stretch out across the floor and up to the ceiling.

Tubes, cables and plastic piping.

A steel compressor. Thin pointers vibrating faintly.

On a shiny, chrome stool lies a cardboard-coloured folder.

A sluggish piston movement is visible under a glass dome.

Flesh-coloured tubes come together in big, twisted bunches and feed into a hole in the wall.

Suddenly a red warning light comes on.

Ingmar bangs on the window, climbs down, scrapes himself on a protruding angle iron, and sucks the wound as he runs to the main entrance.

He looks in through the glass doors and sees a nurse who is standing talking to an elderly couple. Ingmar knocks on the glass with his wedding ring. She looks towards him and he beckons. She looks away and carries on talking, but he knocks again and waves.

She comes out and asks him what he wants. Hugging her cardigan round her. Freckles sprinkled across her nose and forehead.

'I'm just wondering how my father is,' says Ingmar, and finds his mouth suddenly so dry that he has to eat a bit of snow from the edge of a plant container.

'Your father?'

'Is he dead?' he asks, scarcely audible. 'Do you know?'

'Which ward is he in?'

'Ward? Surely you'd know if anyone had died today.'

'Today?'

Ingmar has to eat some more snow.

'Erik Bergman, that's his name.'

'Nothing like that has happened today,' she says gravely.

'But just now? It could have happened right this minute, without you knowing, couldn't it?'

'Come in and we can find out what . . .'

'Find out? You mean go through some bloody pile of papers?'

She lowers her eyes, pauses for a few seconds, then turns and goes in.

Ingmar decides to get the chocolate and leave it at reception. He goes back to the car, gets into the driver's seat and shuts the door to keep the snow out.

He is so cold that he is shaking. He starts to feel a prickling in his hands and arms.

He notices the key in the ignition and then shuts his eyes.

His heart is beating far too fast.

The seat springs creak as he pulls his knees up in front of the steering wheel. He curls into a ball as best he can. Breathes against the fabric of his trousers.

The wind whistles across the roof of the car and round its body. Gusts even more fiercely for a moment, then catches its breath and falls silent.

The car gradually warms up and Ingmar relaxes.

His breathing calms down, his muscles cautiously soften.

Suddenly, there is a huge jolt and his knees bash into his mouth. The front has run up against the muddy bank. Water washes over the planking of the ferry's deck.

He sees the women going ashore, being helped with their hay-cart.

'Come on then, you chump.'

'Eh?'

Ingmar looks up. The car windows are misted a solid grey. It is dark inside the car. Even so, the air he exhales shows up against the black dashboard.

Somebody gives an underwater shout.

The driver's door is opened and snow falls off the car roof. A man in pale grey clothes is standing there.

'You can't sit here,' he says.

'No,' Ingmar responds.

'You'll freeze to death.'

The man gives a faint smile as Ingmar tries to pull the door closed. He holds it steady and bends forward.

'You get off home now,' he says.

'Just got to find out how Father is.'

The door slams shut, Ingmar closes his eyes, grits his teeth and waits.

'It didn't hurt,' he thinks.

When his father gripped the tops of his arms, shook him, and shouted that he was of no significance.

His father righted the bicycle, pulled it from the

ditch, out of the meadow grass and obstinate brush-wood. And started wheeling it along the straight, dirt road.

Once he noticed Ingmar was running after him, he got onto the bicycle and pedalled off.

Ingmar remembers finally having to stop, panting furiously, his legs heavy and shaking.

He saw his father disappear on the bicycle.

And then the empty road through the forest.

Tossing fescue and fireweed and nettles in the shade; flies, horseflies and a shimmering dragonfly.

Ingmar stood staring, but when his father did not return, he went back to the landing stage. He waited a while and then walked a little way downstream.

Stopped where the river grew swift and deep.

He saw the taut, onward sweeping film over the darkness. Decided he would swim across to get home, knowing that he would not have the strength, the water would be too cold, the currents too strong.

Legs trembling, he walked round the great boulder and suddenly found himself facing a young woman with sturdy arms and wide hips. She had filled her apron pocket with stones, a crutch lay on the ground; her eyes were black and the white sky was reflected in them like frosted glass.

Ingmar ran up the hill and through a patch of forest.

When he emerged onto the dirt road again, he saw his father cycling towards him. With a smile, as if nothing had happened while he was away.

Ingmar sat down in the middle of the road, buried his face in his hands and cried as if he would never be able to stop.

The father should carefully have picked up his son from the road and sat himself down in the ditch.

There would have been no need to speak, to rock. If only he had sat on the edge of the forest with his youngest son in his arms.

Ingmar opens his eyes as he hears a knock on the car window. Through the misted windscreen he sees fluttering movements.

The car door is opened and a man of his own age looks in and says hello. His white doctor's coat flaps in the wind. Snowflakes fly above his head on haphazard courses.

'I've just come from Erik Bergman. His temperature's still high, but he's doing fine.'

'You needn't lie just to . . .'

'No, he's fine.'

Ingmar thanks him, shakes his hand at length, and suddenly feels his eyes stinging.

'You can go and see him now,' says the doctor. 'He'd like that, I'm quite sure.'

'Well, I'm not.'

'Don't you want to come in with me and . . .'

'No, I've got to go,' replies Ingmar, and turns his face away.

13

In the thirteenth glass jar there are suddenly two people walking. As transparent as the space around them.

They pass the hotel bar on the way to the restaurant. Soundlessly across the fitted carpet.

A man with a tired, tanned face gets up from his armchair. He accosts them, wanting to offer Ingmar his congratulations.

'Thanks very much.'

The man runs his fingers through his thick hair, laughs and says a few more words in his Swabian dialect.

Ingmar and Käbi walk on, following the curving glass wall towards the dining room.

'What was that about?'

'Your latest Oscar,' she says.

'I thought he meant . . .'

'You're fixated with the premiere.'

'Yes, I thought he must have heard something.'

'People haven't even had time to get to the cinema yet,' she says.

'I know,' he sighs.

'The first few may have arrived, but . . .'

'I'm just a little stressed.'

Käbi speaks to the head waiter and they are shown through the empty dining room to a secluded table.

Ingmar looks out of the big window, but feels compressed by the dizzying alpine scenery.

And yet their surroundings fit snugly into the curvature of the wine glass.

A ludicrous miniature in a souvenir globe, with snow on the pointed mountain tops, black forest and wooden chalets.

'What they write tomorrow doesn't matter,' she says. 'It's a masterpiece.'

'But dreary,' he says.

'Terribly dreary,' she jokes.

'Couldn't we just sever all contact with Sweden this week? Completely and utterly?'

She nods and looks out of the window.

'What's the matter?' he says. 'Is it Daniel?'

'No, it's just . . . That's the way I am,' she answers with a smile. 'I start worrying whenever he's out of my sight.'

Ingmar holds a short strip of film up to the nervous candle flame.

Four identical pictures: a skinny, blotchy baby on a blanket with the municipal crest in one corner.

The little boy is still in the shape of the womb. His knees drawn up and his little fists pressed against his chest.

Ingmar's eyes rest on the swollen testicles between the baby's thighs, gleaming in the flickering light.

'Maybe we should have brought him with us, after all.'

'No, he's too little,' says Käbi. 'I'll ring Bärbel in the morning and find out if his temperature's down.'

'Can't you ring tonight?'

'It's only an ordinary cold.'

'But I was thinking: all the reviews will be out tomorrow,' he says, putting the strip of film into a jar. 'I'd only start imagining Bärbel had said something that you were trying to hide from me, etcetera etcetera.'

She nods, but doesn't meet his imploring gaze.

'You know me.'

'No,' she replies faintly. 'I know that you lie down on your back, clasp your hands together on your chest and go to sleep at half past ten.'

'Is that all?' he laughs.

She has to suppress a smile.

He puts the menu down on the table.

'Shall we order?' she asks.

'If there is anything edible.'

'Fillet of lamb.'

'Where's that?'

'There,' she says, pointing. 'And this is veal.'

Ingmar tips the contents of the box onto the table, puts back the five tin soldiers and starts lining up the animals: a horse and a pig, two ewes, a lamb and a ram. The black goat and a cow.

'They should all be there by now,' he says, looking at his watch again. 'Outside the Röda Kvarn or in the foyer.'

'Gunnar, Max, Ingrid, Gunnel, Allan . . .'

'No, not Gunnel,' smiles Ingmar, removing one of the ewes. 'She never gets above second gear, so she won't be there yet.'

He chews his thumbnail.

'Do you even know if your father was planning to go?'

'I've put some tickets aside, but . . .'

He looks at the serving dish on which there is a thin slice of veal fillet with crushed black pepper.

'Let's think about something else now,' suggests Käbi cautiously.

'Yes.'

'You're not to worry about what he does.'

'Let me just say that I do realize it might be quite a strain for him to go to a premiere.'

With the lingering taste of compost from the Styrian wine still in his mouth, he wipes condensation from the glass with his thumb and sees the waiter coming in.

A flat plate is placed in front of him. Lamb fillet, diced bacon, a sprig of thyme and three piped peaks of potato purée with truffles.

The waiter carefully pours the madeira, lime and blackberry sauce, gets a splash of pink on his arm and retreats.

'You've stopped talking now,' Käbi says. 'You came here, but you're there all the same, at a premiere that . . .'

'It's not something I want,' he interrupts her with a laugh. 'It creeps up from behind, the whole time, almost like Chopin's *Barcarolle*.'

He sees Käbi performing in Oslo, the zip at the back of her dress opening a centimetre or two with every new passage.

'But I came with you,' says Käbi. 'I came with you to Switzerland to . . .'

Ingmar puts the heavy glass lid on the jam jar. The green ring of rubber seals it tight. Käbi's voice fails to penetrate it; she stops talking and goes red under the eyes. Feels offended yet holds her chin high.

'They're all sitting there in the auditorium now, all the guests, all the critics,' he says.

She nods and moves the jar aside.

He tries to take deep breaths.

Is aware of a sombre bouquet of Merlot rising from the black bottle from Saint Emilion.

The anxiety churns heavily in the pit of his stomach.

'Don't you want any?'

'Let me just . . .'

His fork prods the sliced meat.

Sinks in and makes a trail through the sauce.

'It'll be interesting for Gunnar to see himself playing a priest,' Käbi says lightly. 'While you see him playing you as a priest and . . .'

'What do the others see?' mumbles Ingmar, meeting his own gaze in a mirror.

'Exactly what I was sitting here wondering.'

He chews rapidly, feels his teeth cutting through the meat, the blood, the salty and sour tastes.

Käbi reads his look and pours him some wine.

'Thanks.'

'Shed for thee,' she says drily.

He tilts the big jar with the thick liquid in the bottom. Käbi shakes her wet sleeve and gives him a tired look through the glass.

'Sorry.'

In another jar he can see an enhanced version of himself, eating vanilla ice cream with movements that are far too rapid.

'Looks delicious,' says Käbi.

He sucks his spoon and nods. Looks at his watch and wipes his mouth.

'Nearly nine.'

He wonders if his father has seen the film, has sat in silence in the taxi to Storgatan. Or if his mother has walked home alone. Maybe had Agda for company. If she is setting out teacups on the eighteenth-century table or describing the film while his father watches television.

'I'll sit here while you go and phone, if you like,' says Käbi.

He gets to his feet, takes a last spoonful of ice cream and then makes his way hurriedly between the round tables in the vast restaurant.

As if ahead of himself, he slips the key into the lock even before the creaking lift comes to a halt.

And as he walks along the silent corridor he is simultaneously inside his hotel room, reaching the yellow sofa and armchairs.

The bleached ridge along the centre of the carpet is there to meet him. The wall lights flow slowly by. The dull gleam of the brass fittings on the doors repeats itself, along with the limited permutations of the mouldings.

He stands with the telephone receiver to his ear at the same time as he turns the key in the lock, opens the door, walks across the fitted pink carpet, sits down in the yellow armchair, lifts the receiver from its cradle and asks to be put through to a number in Sweden.

His heart is hammering.

But quietens when no one answers.

He sits there for a while and looks out at the dark grey Alps, streaked with white.

It occurs to him that he could ring Lenn and ask who came to the premiere.

He picks up the receiver once more, asks the receptionist to try the number again.

And as he hears it ringing at the other end, he

remembers the way he lined up his glass jars.

On the shady stretch of gravel behind the vicarage.

He lies down and tries to make out something through the shifting hues, but the corridor of small, enclosed worlds turns away.

Seems to curve and darken.

Heaves this way and that.

Until the refractions suddenly cancel each other out and Ingmar is forced to open his eyes.

He's back, alone in this hotel room in St Moritz.

While Käbi sits in the restaurant, eating her crème caramel.

And the rings continue, one after another.

'Bergman,' his father answers, and gives a sigh as he sits down at his desk.

'It's Ingmar.'

'We've literally just walked through the door.'

'Shall I ring back later?'

'It's Putte,' says his father, speaking at some distance from the receiver.

'I can talk to him,' whispers Ingmar's mother.

Ingmar stands up, scratches his throat.

'I have seen your film,' says his father.

'There was no obligation.'

'What can I say?' he goes on. 'I remember you trying to get me to read the script, but . . . I am glad I didn't.'

'Yes, maybe it was . . .'

'I shall be brief – Mother wants to say a few words.'

'The film was just a way of trying to . . .'

'Ingmar,' his father interrupts. 'I'm touched, actually. It was . . . We can talk about it next time we meet, but I have to admit I would never have thought that you . . .'

He clears his throat; his wife says something in the background and he exchanges a few words with her.

'Well, as I said to Mother on the way home: it was a little like being a curate at the Forsbacka ironworks again. It was my church, it was my loneliness – I shan't exaggerate, but . . . I want you to know that I am grateful to have a portrayal of that period, as it were.'

Ingmar's hands are shaking as the receiver is handed over to his mother. He sits down and barely listens as she tells him with suppressed elation that the film will probably be lost on the average audience.

Käbi's strappy shoes are on the floor in front of the yellow sofa and her tights are in the waste-paper basket.

'But everybody was there,' his mother says. 'Gunnar Björnstrand and Max von Sydow came and said hello, and Ingrid Thulin in a gorgeous . . .'

She stops as Ingmar's father says something in the background.

'Yes, I'm just going to make some tea,' she replies.

Ingmar replaces the receiver and then sits with his face in his hands. Feels his exhaled breath tickle his eyelids. Then the cooler draught as his lungs fill.

'He didn't go to the premiere, did he?' Käbi asks.

'Father? Oh, he was there all right.'

The window panes creak a little as the wind gets up.

'He said he was touched,' Ingmar says quietly.

Käbi flushes and is unable to hide her annoyance.

'I can't take much more of this.'

'Of what?'

'I can't bear your constant lying,' she says.

'No, truly, Father said the priest was a portrayal of him, from his time in Forsbacka, when he . . .'

'He said the priest was a portrayal of him?' she asks sceptically.

'Yes, and he's quite right,' responds Ingmar.

'Well if so, where does that leave you?'

'I haven't thought that far,' he says. 'If I'm not the priest, I must . . . No, I really don't know.'

'But you're always incredibly particular about who you identify with.'

'It's just . . .'

Ingmar stands up and sees the landscape changing colour. Feels the draught at floor level, circling from behind his legs and then out.

The fir forest darkens swiftly.

And the grey folds of the rock face turn a soft bottle-green.

He gets to the big window just as the Alps begin to glow, as ethereally as in a damaged photograph.

'Because after all, you've got to be someone,' she repeats.

Ingmar feels as if he is about to fall; he gropes, grabs hold of the curtain and hears the rod squeak in its fittings.

'I don't know,' he whispers.

The peaked massif rises in the darkness like pale pink glass, rugged and illuminated from within.

'There is one person, of course, who loves the priest just as a child would,' says Käbi. 'A person you despise, but who really only wants to

Afterword

Despite the fact that *The Director* is a novel and primarily a product of my imagination (with no claims to truth other than artistic ones) I feel tempted to acknowledge and thank my most important sources.

Along with the extensive biographical and fictional material provided by Bergman himself, I have read his mother Karin's diary and letters, his father Erik's memoirs, his wife Käbi Laretei's autobiographical works and the writings of various other family members.

I would also like to single out Maaret Koskinen, Leif Zern and Birgit Linton-Malmfors; for the long section dealing with the filming of *Winter Light*, I have drawn above all on Vilgot Sjöman's diary with Ingmar Bergman. Perhaps that is why I wanted to thank Vilgot in a special way, by allowing him to plod into the limelight as a garden gnome in Ingmar's bed.

That will have to do. I have decided not to add a bibliography of the vast amount of material that has passed through me and left its mark in this story, just as I leave out any account of the preparatory studies I undertook – visits to film locations, homes and other significant settings – or of how I found my way by sometimes illicit means into the rooms I wanted to see, since in other places I have relied entirely on my own imagination.

Alexander Ahndoril